SO-CFQ-480

## THE RIDDLE GAME

**WHAT WAS FARMER GILES OF HAM'S FULL LATIN NAME?**

**WHEN MELKOR WENT INTO THE VOID, WHAT WAS HE SEEKING?**

**HOW WERE FRODO AND BILBO RELATED?**

**WHAT DO THE INITIALS J.R.R. STAND FOR?**

Got them all right? Then you're ready to match wits with Bilbo and Gollum and countless Tolkein fans in solving the 1001 memory-stumping questions in—

# THE TOLKIEN QUIZ BOOK

*(See answers below)*

Aegidius Ahenobarbus Julius Agricola de Hammo
The Imperishable Flame
They were first *and* second cousins
John Ronald Reuel

# THE TOLKIEN QUIZ BOOK*

## 1001 Questions About Tolkien's Tales of Middle-earth and Other Fantasies

by
**Bart Andrews**

with

**Bernie Zuber**

A SIGNET BOOK

**NEW AMERICAN LIBRARY**

TIMES MIRROR

*This book is dedicated to
the Wallington Book Mart
of Wallington, New Jersey,
where this book was born,
and to all Tolkien fans
who have waited
patiently for it.*

 SIGNET TRADEMARK REG. U.S. PAT. OFF. AND FOREIGN COUNTRIES
REGISTERED TRADEMARK—MARCA REGISTRADA
HECHO EN CHICAGO, U.S.A.

SIGNET, SIGNET CLASSICS, MENTOR, PLUME and MERIDIAN BOOKS
are published by The New American Library, Inc.,
1301 Avenue of the Americas, New York, New York 10019

First Printing, February, 1979

1 2 3 4 5 6 7 8 9

PRINTED IN THE UNITED STATES OF AMERICA

# Notes from Middle-Hollywood

"A Tolkien quiz book??" I repeated incredulously to my agent Trupin over the phone. "That's impossible! There's no way I can do it. I don't know enough about the man and his work. And you know how volatile those Tolkien fans are. They'll roast me over coals if I leave out so much as one measly accent mark! Whose idea was this anyway?"

"Yours, client," he reminded me. "Remember, you came back from a picnic last Labor Day bubbling over with the idea?"

"That's what I said—it's a great idea. And besides, you know how I love a good barbecue."

I put down the receiver and stared out the window a moment. *Tolkien, eh? I think he wrote* The Hobbit, *or* The Habit, *or something like that. Didn't I read it at N.Y.U. during a panty raid? It was fun (and so was the book). But enough of this daydreaming, Andrews. Better put on your best elf outfit and get busy. The dwarves are waiting.*

Several months and 1,001 questions later, the manuscript was completed. But I wouldn't have gotten farther than 101 questions without a *lot* of help:

Let me thank Christopher Gilson, an expert in Elvish who put together a few of these quizzes; Merritt Thompson, who created the beautiful Tengwar calligraphy for the book; Bill Welden, another Tolkien aficionado and a contributor to the forthcoming book *An Introduction to Elvish*, who checked the manuscript for accuracy (and I *do* mean checked it; and Rick Israel, who supplied ideas and acted as a sounding board for most of the material.

Most of all, I want to thank Bernie Zuber, founder of The Tolkien Fellowships, and editor and publisher of its journal, *The Westmarch Chronicle*. Bernie did a masterful research job and managed to complete it even while helping to promote the new Ralph Bakshi film of *The Lord of the Rings* in his capacity as co-director (with his wife, Teny) of fan relations. Anyone interested in contacting Bernie can reach him through Box 8853, San Marino, California 91108—if you want to join his wonderful organization or just talk about this book.

In the meantime, enjoy the quizzes, and let us know if you'd like to see Volume Two.

—BART ANDREWS

*Los Angeles, California*
*August 1, 1978*

# QUESTIONS

# 1. HOBBITS

1. What was Tobold Hornblower's claim to fame?
2. Who were the Fairbairns of the Towers?
3. What colors were hobbits particularly fond of?
4. What showed that the hobbits of the Eastfarthing were of the Stoor breed?
5. Who was the first hobbit to wear the Ring?
6. What did the Hobbitish word *"hlothran"* mean?
7. Who were Marcho and Blanco?
8. What breed of hobbits had the most contact with Dwarves?
9. What were hobbits called in Westron?
10. Who was the only real official in the Shire, and what were his duties?

## 2. THE SHIRE

1. What was the Three-Farthing Stone?
2. Name four inns of the Shire and give their locations.
3. What was the name of Farmer Maggot's farm?
4. Name its major crop.
5. What was the principal township of the Shire?
6. Where did Fredegar Bolger and his rebels hide from Lotho Sackville-Baggins?
7. Give the dimensions of the Shire in leagues.
8. What was peculiar about hobbit architecture?
9. On what day of the year was the Horn of the Mark blown in Buckland to announce bonfires and feastings?
10. Who built Brandy Hall?

# 3. SAY IT IN ELVISH

Fill in the missing word in each Elvish phrase. Translations of each phrase have been supplied to aid you.

*Quenya phrases:*
1. *Elen síla —— omentielvo.* (A star shines on the hour of our meeting.)
2. *Sí man i —— nin enquantuva?* (Who now shall refill the cup for me?)
3. *Nai hiruvalye Valimar; nai —— hiruva.* (Maybe thou shalt find Valimar; maybe even thou shalt find it.)
4. *Auta i ——!* (The night is passing!)
5. *Sinome maruvan ar —— tenn' Ambar-metta!* (In this place will I abide, and my heirs, unto the ending of the world!)

*Sindarin phrases:*
6. *Ai na —— Dúnadan, mae govannen!* (Ah, at last Dúnadan, well met!)
7. *O galadhremmin ——, Fanuilos, le linnathon.* (From the tree-woven lands of Middle-earth, Snow-white, I sing to thee.)
8. *Dor —— i-Guinar.* (Land of the Dead that Live.)
9. *Celebrimbor o Eregion —— i thiw hin.* (Celebrimbor of Hollin drew these signs.)
10. *Ónen i- —— Edain, ú-chebin —— anim.* (I gave hope to the Edain, I have kept no hope for myself.)

# 4. THERE . . .

1. Which rooms in Bilbo's hobbit-hole had windows?
2. How old was Bilbo when his adventure started?
3. How did Bilbo ignore Gandalf?
4. What did Gandalf scratch on Bilbo's door?
5. On what day of the week was the Unexpected Party?
6. Name the thirteen dwarves who appeared at Bilbo's door (in the order of their appearance).
7. What word did Bilbo not like the "sound" of?
8. Who didn't say "at your service"?
9. Who asked for raspberry jam and apple-tart?
10. Which dwarves brought these instruments: fiddles, flutes, drum, clarinets, viols, harp?

# 5. . . . AND BACK AGAIN

1. What did Bilbo say that was roughly equivalent to the term "out of the frying pan and into the fire"?
2. Who acted as a counsellor and messenger to Thorin?
3. What did Bilbo see flying over Mirkwood as he poked his head above the treetops?
4. What was the favorite drink of the king of the Wood-elves?
5. What reason did Bilbo give Smaug for Bilbo's inclusion in the Dwarves' expedition?
6. Name three compliments bestowed on Smaug by Bilbo.
7. Who killed Bolg?
8. What gift did Bilbo offer the king of the Wood-elves?
9. What commotion was going on when Bilbo returned to Bag End?
10. Who came with Gandalf when he visited Bilbo some years after the adventure?

# 6. THE RIDDLE GAME

1. Who asked the first riddle, Bilbo or Gollum?
2. What is the answer to this riddle: "Thirty white horses on a red hill, first they champ, then they stamp, then they stand still"?
3. What was "an eye in a blue face"?
4. Who or what was "three-legs"?
5. What was Gollum's first guess when Bilbo said, "What have I got in my pocket?"?
6. To what riddle did Gollum answer the correct response "eggses"?
7. "This thing all things devours." What is it?
8. What was it that Bilbo had meant to say when he accidentally gave the correct answer to the ninth riddle?
9. When Gollum paddled back to his island, what was he going to look for?
10. Which passage from Gollum's lake led to the back-door?

# 7. CHAPTER SEVEN

1. After the Seven Fathers of the Dwarves were created by Aulë, what was Ilúvatar's command?
2. What ravine was barred by seven gates?
3. What Third Age city had seven gates?
4. What were the Seven Hoards?
5. Name the seven rivers of southern Gondor.
6. Give another name for the Seven Stars.
7. What major character in *The Lord of the Rings* had seven toes on each foot?
8. What ultimately happened to the Seven Rings of the Dwarves?
9. What were the Seven Stones?
10. What great hall was on the Seventh Level of Khazad-dûm?

# 8. GOLLUM

1. What kind of creature was Gollum?
2. What was his original name?
3. Who was it that Gollum strangled to steal the Ring?
4. How did Gollum explain his possession of the Ring to Gandalf?
5. What was Gollum's favorite meat when he could get it?
6. How many teeth did he have?
7. Where did Gollum live when Bilbo met him?
8. What did Gollum call the sun?
9. What was Gollum's promise to Frodo?
10. What was Gollum saying as he fell into the Cracks of Doom?

# 9. ELVISH MATCH

Match the Sindarin colors with their nearest English equivalents.

| | | | |
|---|---|---|---|
| 1. *Baran* | | a. White |
| 2. *Calen* | | b. Silver |
| 3. *Caran* | | c. Silver-grey |
| 4. *Celeb* | | d. Grey |
| 5. *Glaur* | | e. Black |
| 6. *Luin* | | f. Blue |
| 7. *Mith* | | g. Green |
| 8. *Mor* | | h. Gold |
| 9. *Nim* | | i. Brown |
| 10. *Thind* | | j. Red |

## 10. BEASTS

1. Whose cats were "proverbial" in their ability to find their way home?
2. Who was Felaróf?
3. Who were the Dumbledors?
4. Name Gwaihir's brother.
5. What horse killed its master by falling on him during the Battle of the Pelennor Fields?
6. What birds of Erebor and Dale could understand Westron?
7. Name Farmer Maggot's three dogs.
8. Who was Roäc?
9. What wild beast was hunted and slain by King Folca of Rohan?
10. What were the names of the four ponies that Frodo, Sam, Merry, and Pippin rode into Bree?

# 11. THE VALAR

Match the Valar with their titles.

1. Manwë
2. Yavanna
3. Tulkas

4. Aulë
5. Varda
6. Námo
7. Vairë

8. Oromë
9. Ulmo
10. Vána

a. Lady of the Stars
b. The Weaver
c. Keeper of the Houses of the Dead
d. Lord of Waters
e. The Ever-young
f. The Giver of Fruits
g. Lord of the Breath of Arda
h. The Valiant
i. Lord of Forests
j. The Master of all Crafts

# 12. THE POET'S CORNER

Fill in the missing words in each of these poems or songs of Middle-earth.

1. "He chanted a song of wizardry,
   Of piercing, ——, of ——"
2. "Gil-galad was an Elven-king.
   Of him ——"
3. "In the willow-meads of Tasarinan I walked in the Spring.
   Ah! the sight and the smell of the Spring in ——"
4. "O! Sweet is the sound of falling rain,
   and the brook that leaps from hill to plain;
   but better than rain or ——
   is ——that ——"
5. "Eärendil was a mariner
   that tarried in ——;
   he built a boat of timber felled
   in —— to journey in"
6. *"O Orofarnë, Lassemista, ——!*
   O Rowan Fair, upon your hair how ——!"
7. "Tree and Flower and leaf and grass,
   ——! ——!
   Hill and water under sky,
   ——! ——!"
8. *"A! Elbereth Gilthoniel!*
   —— *penna míriel*
   *O —— elenath*
   *Gilthoniel, A! Elbereth"*
9. "In joy thou hast lived. ——!"
10. "He sought her ever, wandering far
    Where —— were thickly strewn,
    By light of moon and ——
    In Frosty heavens shivering"

# 13. OUT OF THE HOBBIT HOLE

1. What hobbit was called "muddy feet" by Tom Bombadil?
2. Name the hobbit who invented the game of golf, and explain how he did it.
3. What was it that the Took family usually hushed up?
4. Give the name of a Shire firm of auctioneers.
5. Which hobbit families lived in Tightfield?
6. To whom did Bilbo leave an empty bookcase, and why?
7. Who was called Cock-Robin, and what was his duty when Frodo and Sam returned to the Shire?
8. What was Tunnelly?
9. What was the Hobbitish nickname for "stay at home"?
10. Give the village and area of the Eastfarthing where the Bolger family lived.

# 14. J. R. R. TOLKIEN

1. Give the names of Tolkien's children in the order in which they were born.
2. In 1954, which of Tolkien's works was performed on the BBC Third Programme?
3. Who was Elaine Griffiths, and why was she important to Tolkien's career?
4. Which two names from Middle-earth are inscribed on Tolkien's grave?
5. In *The Father Christmas Letters*, for what years did Tolkien illustrate these scenes: Father Christmas packing gifts, a party of Snowboys and Polar-cubs, the Aurora Borealis at the North Pole, and the North Polar Bear falling down the stairs?
6. Which of his creations was Tolkien referring to when he said, ". . . it grows like a seed in the dark out of the leaf-mould of the mind"?
7. W. H. Auden once told Tolkien that his voice was like that of Gandalf. What was Tolkien reading when he inspired this comment?
8. When Tolkien was a child, what nickname did he give a Sarehole farmer who chased him for picking mushrooms?
9. In the *Silmarillion Calendar* for 1978, which of Tolkien's own illustrations are used for the months January, March, June, and September?
10. What music was performed for the Tolkiens' golden wedding anniversary party at Merton College in 1966?

# 15. SAM

1. Give Sam's full name.
2. Sam followed in his father's footsteps. What profession did they share?
3. Where did Sam and his father, Ham Gamgee, live?
4. How did Sam become involved in Frodo's journey?
5. Whom did Sam very much want to see?
6. What did Sam call Gollum?
7. What did Sam decide to do when he thought that Frodo had been killed by Shelob?
8. Why was Sam able to rescue Frodo single-handed from Cirith Ungol?
9. Whom did Sam marry?
10. How many times did Sam become Mayor of the Shire after the War of the Ring?

# 16. IN FANGORN FOREST

1. Give both the Elvish and English names of the last three of the First Ents that walked in the woods before the Darkness.
2. Who was Wandlimb?
3. What Ent was called Quickbeam, and explain why?
4. What did Treebeard call Isengard?
5. Treebeard's manner of speaking, with its "hrum, hroom," was based on the voice of what living person?
6. What was the Sindarin name for the Ents?
7. According to Treebeard, who were the Free peoples?
8. What did Treebeard tell Merry and Pippin was the original name of Lothlórien?
9. What happened when Treebeard held his hands over two vessels on his table?
10. What became of the Entwives?

# 17. THE AINULINDALË

1. By what other name was Ilúvatar, the creator, better known in the Third Age of Middle-earth?
2. Who were the Ainur?
3. What did Ilúvatar show the Ainur after the Great Music?
4. Which Ainu disrupted the harmony of the Great Music?
5. What name was given to the first of the Ainur that descended into the world, and what did it mean?
6. What were the *fanar*?
7. Who were the Children of Ilúvatar, and in what order were they conceived?
8. What was Melkor's ambition concerning the Children of Ilúvatar?
9. When Melkor went into the void, what was he seeking?
10. Who was the chief instrument of the second theme Ilúvatar raised against the discord of Melkor?

## 18. VILLAINS

1. What follower of Sauron had forgotten his own name, and what was he called instead?
2. During the Siege of Gondor and the Battle of the Pelennor Fields, who was called Captain of Sauron?
3. Describe what could be seen when the Lord of the Nazgûl flung back his head.
4. How many Black Riders were there?
5. In the War of the Ring, who was Gothmog?
6. Give the language and meaning of the name *Nazgûl*.
7. By whom was the Black Speech spoken in the Third Age?
8. Who were the Haradrim and where did they come from?
9. Who was the Witch King of Angmar?
10. Name the grandsons of Castamir the Usurper who led the Corsairs against Gondor.

## 19. MONSTERS

1. Where did the Watcher in the Water live?
2. Name a lord of the Balrogs.
3. Describe the two Watchers at the gate of the Tower of Cirith Ungol.
4. What was special about the Olog-hai trolls of southern Mirkwood and northern Mordor?
5. Who was Ungoliant?
6. What did Ungoliant eat and always hunger for?
7. What was the name of the great wolf of Angband who bit off Beren's hand with the Silmaril?
8. About what sea monster was there a poem written in the Red Book?
9. What monster lived under Cirith Ungol?
10. Give a description of the Balrog that fought with Gandalf at Khazad-dûm.

# 20. PLACE SETTINGS

1. On what island was the kingdom of Númenor founded?
2. Describe the course of the Withywindle.
3. What were the Mounds of Mundburg?
4. What was Caras Galadon?
5. What were the Pinnath Gelin?
6. In what mountains was Nimrodel lost?
7. What separated the Shire from the Old Forest for a distance of at least twenty miles?
8. Name the six rivers of Ossiriand that flowed into the River Gelion, from north to south.
9. What were the Caves of the Forgotten and where were they located?
10. What was three hundred miles north of the Shire, and who lived there?

# 21. BATTLES

Match the opposing forces, or armies, and then match them with the battles listed below.

1. Durin's Folk
2. Gondor, Lindon, and Rivendell
3. Rohan and Fangorn
4. Dale and Erebor
5. Balchoth and Orcs
6. Wainriders
7. Eldacar's Army
8. Mordor
9. Gondor and Rohan
10. Orcs

a. Gondor
b. The Last Alliance
c. Éotheód and Gondor
d. Dúnedain of Arnor
e. Easterlings
f. Harad
g. Orcs of Azog
h. Dunlendings and Orcs
i. Army of the Witch-king of Angmar
j. Castamir's Army

A. Battle of Azanulbizar
B. Battle of Dargorlad
C. Battle of Dale
D. Battle of Fornost
E. Battle of the Camp
F. Battle of the Crossings of Poros
G. Battle of the Hornburg
H. Battle of the Field of Celebrant
I. Battle of the Gladden Fields
J. Battle of the Crossings of Erui

## 22. COMPOUNDING IT

Translate the Elvish compounds by filling in the blanks.

### *Quenya compounds:*

1. *Sorontar*: "King of ———"
2. *Oiolossë*: "——— white"
3. *Taniquetil*: "High-white-———"
4. *Tyelpetéma*: "palatal ———"
5. *Ilúvatar*: "——— of All"

### *Sindarin compounds:*

6. *Fëanor*: "Spirit of ———"
7. *Celebrindal*: "Silver-———"
8. *Sarn Athrad*: "Stony ———"
9. *Angband*: "———Prison"
10. *Pelargir*: "Garth of Royal ———"

## 23. SHIRE RECKONING

1. List the months of the Shire calendar in order.
2. What time measurement were the hobbits lacking when they were still a wandering people?
3. On what day did the Shire week begin?
4. What month name of the Shire calendar was a focus of derision among the people of Bree?
5. Name the four months whose names were the same in the Bree calendar as in the Shire calendar.
6. By how many days was the Shire calendar in advance of our 20th-century calendar?
7. Name the days of the week in the Shire calendar at the time of the War of the Ring.
8. Which of those days was considered a holiday, with evening feasts, and to which of our days did it correspond?
9. Which days remained outside the months in the Shire calendar?
10. Give the full expression used as a jest which referred to a nonexistent day.

## 24. WEAPONS

1. What swords were forged from meteoric iron?
2. What was Aiglos, and what did it mean?
3. Name King Theoden's sword.
4. Who forged Narsil?
5. Describe the two weapons that were called Grond.
6. Who was given the sword Caudimordax?
7. Who bore the sword Aranrúth?
8. What two weapons were called Biter and Beater by the Orcs?
9. What was Belthronding and whose weapon was it?
10. Who used a whip at the bridge of Khazad-dûm?

# 25. TOLKIEN TEASERS

1. What is the *full* title of *The Lord of the Rings*?
2. What was The Great Journey?
3. Who were the *peredhil*, and what choice were they given?
4. What did Thain Peregrin bring with him to Gondor in the Fourth Age?
5. Who was William Huggins?
6. What is Blooting?
7. Who were Paksu and Valkotukka, and what did the names mean?
8. Who was the herald of Gil-Galad?
9. How were the ships of the Teleri drawn to Aman?
10. Who commanded an army of hunters, herdsmen, and villagers from Anfalas?

# 26. ARCHITECTURE OF MIDDLE-EARTH

1. Where was the Dome of Stars?
2. What was the name of the city of the Eldar in Eregion?
3. Give the name of the Great Hall of Feasts in Minas Tirith.
4. Identify the Chamber of Records of Khazad-dûm.
5. How many arches were there on the bridge of Mitheithel?
6. Who built the Argonath?
7. Give the name and location of the building having these characteristics: circular base five hundred feet wide, walls five hundred feet high and fifty feet thick, topped by a silver dome.
8. What was the Endless Stair?
9. What was built by Finrod in the Caverns of Narog?
10. Where was the Hall of Fire?

# 27. GONDOR

1. Which king of Gondor rebuilt Minas Anor and began the custom of living in it during the summer?
2. Who was the grandson of the Steward Faramir and what was he noted for?
3. What policy was adopted by the following kings of Gondor: Taranon Falastur, Eärnil I, Ciryandil, and Hyarmendacil I?
4. When did the Stewards become the rulers of Gondor?
5. Who was the throne of Gondor saved for?
6. Who in Gondor finished something later kept by the hobbits at Great Smials?
7. What city of Gondor was built over the river Anduin?
8. When did Anórien become more important than Ithilien?
9. Name the main city of Belfalas on the coast of Gondor.
10. Who was the fourth Ruling Steward of Gondor?

# 28. "FARMER GILES OF HAM"

1. Give Farmer Giles of Ham's full Latin name.
2. What question was put to the Four Wise Clerks of Oxenford?
3. Besides gunpowder, what did Farmer Giles stuff into his blunderbuss?
4. What cry did Garm, Farmer Giles's dog, very often utter?
5. After Giles chased off a giant, the King sent him a sword commonly known as Tailbiter. What was its Latin name?
6. What, in past years, had been served at the King's Christmas Feast, and what was served instead in the days of Giles?
7. After the dragon had been wounded by Giles, what did he promise the villagers?
8. What was the dragon's remark when Giles threatened to hang his skin from the church steeple?
9. Who rescued Giles from the king's men?
10. After Giles became King Ægidius Draconarius, what was a long walk at his court?

## 29. WHO . . .

1. ... tarried in Arvernien?
2. ... was the mother of Boromir and Faramir?
3. ... died in battle in the two hundred and fifty-second year of his life?
4. ... walked in on Barley Butterbur without knocking?
5. ... searched Bag End for treasure?
6. ... appeared to Frodo as a shining white figure?
7. ... opened an ivory door with a crystal key?
8. ... found the One Ring while fishing?
9. ... cast one of the Silmarils into the sea?
10. ... was sent by Círdan on an errand to Rivendell?

## 30. TRUE OR FALSE?

1. Námo was a Dwarf.
2. Barahir was the uncle of Baragund.
3. Mûmak is another name for Oliphaunt.
4. Hirluin of the Green Hills was an Elf.
5. Tol Galen was a mountain.
6. The Edain were called Elf-friends.
7. The gates of the seven levels of Minas Tirith faced different directions.
8. Nokes was a hobbit from Bywater.
9. Friday was the last day of the week in the Shire.
10. When Andúril was reforged it was entirely covered with runes.

# 31. THE TOLKIEN CONNECTION

How were these people associated with Tolkien?

1. Barbara Remington

a. First employee of publisher Allen & Unwin to read *The Hobbit* in 1936

2. Donald Wollheim

b. Approached Tolkien in 1957 about a project for a film of *The Lord of the Rings*

3. Joy Hill

c. Artist who designed the first covers for the Ballantine paperbacks in 1965

4. Forrest J Ackerman

d. One of the members of the T. C., B. S.

5. William Elvin

e. Editor at Ace Books who initiated the "unauthorized" paperback editions of *The Lord of the Rings* in 1965

6. E. V. Gordon

f. Employee of Allen & Unwin publishers who took care of Tolkien's fan mail (and other related matters)

7. Susan Dagnall

g. English stage and film actor who made a recording of *The Hobbit* for Argo Records

(Continued on page 33)

| | |
|---|---|
| 8. Nicol Williamson | h. Worked with Tolkien on a translation of *Sir Gawain and the Green Knight* |
| 9. J. Madelener | i. German artist whose painting "The Mountain Spirit," seen by Tolkien on a postcard, inspired the creation of Gandalf |
| 10. R. Q. Gilson | j. Sang "The Road Goes Ever On" songs on the Caedmon record album and at public performances |

## 32. WHICH ONE DOESN'T BELONG?

Select the entry that should not be included, and explain why.

1. Aramanth, Rorimac, Ferumbas, Ragnor, Rowan
2. Edrahil, Mahtan, Elwë, Ereinion, Eärendur
3. Brego, Egalmoth, Fram, Imrahil, Astaldo
4. Aulë, Eonwë, Manwë, Oromë, Vairë
5. Farin, Frár, Flói, Lóni, Forn
6. Ancalagon, Bregalad, Bumpkin, Gwaihir, Rochallor
7. Belthil, Herugrim, Illuin, Rothinzil, Blotmath
8. Azog, Gorbag, Gorbulas, Mauhúr, Shagrat
9. *Elanor, Simbelmynë, Elenya, Nimloth, Niphredil*
10. Asphodel, Sigismond, Garm, Déor, Gilly

## 33. TRICKY TOLKIEN

1. What is the connection between one of the star performers in the film *The Wizard of Oz* and certain inhabitants of Middle-earth?
2. What does a basket for seed have in common with an inhabitant of Middle-earth?
3. What does a Hindu goddess have to do with a leading character in *The Lord of the Rings*?
4. Why is the answer to the above question an ironic coincidence?
5. What possible connection could there be between a piano in Ramallah, outside Jerusalem, and Tolkien?
6. Name an American university which has something in common with a place in Middle-earth.
7. What Greek and Latin word for the northernmost part of the habitable world is the same as an element of Elvish?
8. What is the connection between an island in the Mediterranean Sea and a word in a language of Middle-earth?
9. What story by C. S. Lewis bears the same name as a place in Middle-earth?
10. What musical term is also the first name of a member of the Baggins family?

## 34. WHO SAID IT?

Recall who said the following, and in what book or volume.

1. "If beggars will not wait at the door but sneak in to try thieving, that is what we do to them."
2. "A snake without fangs may crawl where he will."
3. "Dangerous! And so am I, very dangerous: more dangerous than anything you will ever meet, unless you are brought alive before the seat of the Dark Lord."
4. "Do not mount on this sea monster!"
5. "I think it is a case for a little gentle treatment now."
6. "We make no doubt in any case, that all the treasure of this worm was stolen from our ancestors."
7. "I have quick ears."
8. "Myths are lies, even though lies breathed through silver."
9. " 'Ere, 'oo are you?"
10. "These cursed Southrons come now marching up the ancient roads to swell the hosts of the Dark Tower."

# 35. BY ANY OTHER NAME

Match the names that belong to the same character.

1. Holdwine
2. Tintallë
3. Ar-Pharazôn
4. Bauglir
5. Yavanna
6. Míriel
7. Brytta
8. Aranel
9. Cúthalion
10. Tulkas

a. Tar-Calion
b. Kémentari
c. Perian
d. Elentári
e. Dior
f. Astaldo
g. Melkor
h. Ar-Zimraphel
i. Beleg
j. Léofa

# 36. TOLKIEN TEST

1. Outside the stories of Middle-earth, where does Tolkien mention Unlight?
2. Name two kings of Gondor whose names form an anagram.
3. Why would no man look upon Cabed Naeramath?
4. What was the Nirnaeth Arnoediad and what did it mean?
5. Who was Fastitocalon?
6. Who was Harry Goatleaf?
7. How long did Gil-galad and Elendil besiege Sauron in Barad-dûr?
8. Give the title of Tolkien's only published play and name the characters in it.
9. What was Scary?
10. Name any three of the five Istari.

# 37. ELVISH

1. Mithrim is a place in Beleriand. But originally the name was closest in meaning to  a) Sindar, b) Grey Havens,  c) Ered Mithrin,  d) Gandalf.
2. The Quenya word "*lasse*" means a) girl, b) leaf, c) snow,  d) sweet.
3. The Sindarin word for hobbits is a) *Holbytla,* b) *Kûd-dûkan,* c) *Peredhil,* d) *Periannath.*
4. Yuldar is a plural noun meaning  a) çups, b) drughts, c) East Elves, d) Christmas Elves.
5. Yavanna is the name of a Vala. It means  a) Autumn Closing In,  b) Giver of Fruits,  c) Queen of the Earth,  d) Summer Goddess.
6. An Elvish name for the Vala called Béma by the Rohirrim because of the sound of his great trumpet is  a) Ulmo,  b), Salmar,  c) Oromë,  d) Boromir.
7. What does the Grey-elven word "*mellon*" mean? a) cantalope,  b) friend,  c) golden,  d) open.
8. Lothlórien means  a) Dreamflower,  b) Valley of Singing Gold,  c) City of Trees,  d) Forest of Golden Leaves.
9. Norbury of the Kings (later called Deadman's Dike) was a translation of  a) Aran Moria,  b) Annúminas,  c) Imladrist,  d) Fornost Erain.
10. How do you say "farewell" in Elvish?  a) Mae govannen,  b) Yé utúvienyes,  c) Namárië,  d) Eglerio.

1. What do the initials "J. R. R." stand for?
2. What is the historical origin of the name "Tolkien," and what did it mean?
3. Give Tolkien's date and place of birth.
4. Who was Isaak?
5. What did T. C., B. S. stand for?
6. Name Tolkien's brother.
7. Who was Lord Roberts?
8. Where did Tolkien see some strange and fascinating names when he was a child, and what language were they in?
9. Name the language invented by Tolkien and Marjorie Incledon.
10. Translate the following Oxford slang words used by Tolkien: Brekker, pragger-jogger, maggers memuger, and the Ugger.

## 39. J. R. R. TOLKIEN: THIS IS YOUR LIFE

1. Who taught Tolkien comparative philology in 1912?
2. How did Tolkien astonish his schoolmates in the King Edward's Debating Society?
3. What did Ronald and Edith throw from the balcony of a Birmingham teashop?
4. What gifts did Ronald and Edith exchange on their birthdays in 1910?
5. What "scene" from his life inspired Tolkien to write about Beren and Lúthien?
6. At what age did Tolkien first become a professor?
7. How did an infant and a bird play a part in his life?
8. What inspired the author to write *Leaf by Niggle*?
9. Although Tolkien claimed he disliked allegories, he wrote at least two of them. Name them.
10. Give the name of the Tolkiens' favorite vacation hotel and its location.

## 40. ON THIS DAY

Match the date and the event.

1. 548 SA

a. The Three Rings are completed in Eregion

2. 1979 TA

b. Battle of Greenfields in which Bandobras Took repels an Orc invasion

3. March 25, 2941 TA

c. Corsairs ravage Pelagir and slay King Minardil

4. 1147 TA

d. Birth of Silmariën, daughter of Tar-Elendil of Númenor

5. January 1, 1919 AD

e. The North Polar Bear falls down the stairs

6. 2793 TA

f. Auction of the effects of the "late" Bilbo Baggins, Esq.

7. 1590 SA

g. Tolkien begins to keep a diary

8. June 22, 1342 SR

h. Bucca of the Marish becomes first Thain of the Shire

9. December 20, 1928 AD

i. The War of the Dwarves and the Orcs begins

10. 1634 TA

j. Chance meeting of Gandalf and Thorin at Bree which greatly influenced subsequent events

## 41. TOLKIEN QUERIES

1. In whom flowed the blood of the Maiar, the Eldar, and the Edain?
2. Who were Aerandir, Erellont, and Falathar?
3. Who was Lock-Bearer, and why was he called that?
4. What was Rhosgobel?
5. Name the hideout of the Rangers of Ithilien.
6. What was Uilos?
7. What was Archet?
8. Who was Star-spray, and why was she called that?
9. The 4th king of Arnor and the 21st king of Gondor had a common name. What was it?
10. Name the son of Beorn.

# 42. ALIASES

Match the names that belong to the same character.

1. Láthspell
2. Erchamion
3. Little Pimple
4. Trahald
5. Saruman
6. Longshanks
7. Túrin
8. Fëanor
9. Lórindol
10. Sauron

a. Elessar
b. Gorthaur
c. Olórin
d. Sméagol
e. Beren
f. Sharkey
g. Curufinwë
h. Lotho
i. Agarwaen
j. Hador

## 43. PICTURE THIS

1. Who illustrated the first American publication of *Smith of Wootton Major*?
2. Which of Tolkien's own illustrations are on the covers of the current 1977 paperback editions of *The Hobbit, The Fellowship of the Ring, The Two Towers,* and *The Return of the King?*
3. In 1949, Tolkien was delighted with the work of what illustrator?
4. What strange birds on the cover of the first Ballantine paperback edition of *The Hobbit* upset Tolkien?
5. Name the main characters, drawn by Jack Gaughan, shown on the covers of the Ace editions of *The Fellowship of the Ring, The Two Towers,* and *The Return of the King.*
6. What is the difference between the American edition and the British edition of the *Bilbo's Last Song* poster?
7. Describe the front and back covers of the one-volume paperback edition of *The Lord of the Rings,* published by Allen & Unwin, and give the illustrator's name.
8. The emblems of what Elves are shown on the gold-colored boxed set of *The Hobbit* and *The Lord of the Rings?*

## 44. TOLKIEN CALENDARS

Match each scene or character with a month (or page) and year of the American editions, then match the result with the illustrator.

1. Tom Bombadil
2. The Fellowship of the Ring
3. Bilbo Comes to the Huts of the Raftelves
4. The Balrog
5. The Mirrormere
6. Moria Gate
7. The Riddle Game
8. Gandalf and Bilbo
9. The Healing of Éowyn
10. Orc Army Marching to Minas Tirith
11. Saruman at Orthanc
12. The Pillars of the Kings

a. January, 1976
b. May, 1973
c. October, 1977
d. September, 1976
e. Centerfold, 1973
f. April, 1977
g. February, 1976
h. Centerfold, 1975
i. April, 1978
j. February, 1975
k. Centerfold, 1976
l. July, 1975
m. October, 1973
n. September, 1975

A. Pauline Baynes
B. Tim and Greg Hildebrandt
C. Tim Kirk
D. J. R. R. Tolkien

# 45. TRUE OR FALSE?

1. Iboriel was one of the Eldar.
2. The Doors of Durin were made by Narvi.
3. Minas Morgul was built by Orcs.
4. Amon Hen was at the southern end of Nen Hithoel.
5. Tailbiter was the name of a sword.
6. Galadriel sang the song of Amroth.
7. Endórë was another name for Middle-earth.
8. Rath Celerdain was in Minas Tirith.
9. Mentha Brandybuck was the grandmother of Marmeadas Brandybuck.
10. Bilbo was Frodo's uncle.

# 46. HOBBIT GENEALOGY

1. Who was Linda Proudfoot's paternal grandfather?
2. Who was the eighth child of Samwise Gamgee, and after whom was she named?
3. Who founded the family of Gardner on the Hill?
4. Who was the tenth child of Gerontius Took?
5. Who was the first son of Elanor the Fair and Fastred of Greenholm, and what was the meaning of his name?
6. Name the tenth Thain from the Took family.
7. Whom did Esmeralda Took marry who was nicknamed "Scattergold"?
8. Name Frodo's great-grandmother from the Hornblower family.
9. What was the nickname of Holman, a Shire gardener, from which a family name was derived?
10. What two sons of Gerontius Took explored the world outside the Shire?

## 47. BILBO

1. Who were Bilbo's parents?
2. What was in Bilbo's nature that he inherited from his mother's family?
3. What did Bilbo call the Elves of Rivendell?
4. How old was Bilbo when he adopted Frodo?
5. What did Bilbo do at the end of his Farewell speech?
6. Where did Bilbo tell Gandalf he had put the One Ring?
7. What nice ending did Bilbo think of for his book?
8. Where did Bilbo go after he left the Shire for the last time?
9. How did Bilbo appear to Frodo as he reached for the One Ring in Rivendell?
10. By the time he sailed from the Grey Havens, how old was Bilbo?

1. Which Dwarves in *The Hobbit* were not of Durin's line?
2. Name the only Dwarf woman ever mentioned in their history.
3. Who were known as the Longbeards?
4. What did the Dwarves call their creator?
5. Who first devised the runes used by the Dwarves and known as the Cirth?
6. What was the name of the Dwarves' language, and who invented it?
7. Give the Dwarvish names of the three mountains over Moria.
8. When the last moon of Autumn and the sun are together in the sky, what day is it for the Dwarves?
9. Give the Sindarin name for the tribe of Dwarves in Beleriand, commonly known as the Petty-Dwarves.
10. What was the first indication that the Dwarves made by Aulë had a life of their own?

## 49. ELROND AND RIVENDELL

1. In what capacity did Elrond take part in the Battle of Dagorlad?
2. What name was given to Elrond and his brother Elros by the Valar, and what did it mean?
3. What was the Sindarin name for Rivendell?
4. What king of Arnor was born and raised at Rivendell?
5. Who was the chief counsellor of Elrond's household?
6. Name the cordial that Elrond gave Gandalf when the Fellowship left Rivendell.
7. Which Elven ring from the First Age was kept at Rivendell?
8. Whom did Elrond marry, and what were the names of the couple's children?
9. During the Council of Elrond, what happened to cause the Elves to cover their ears?
10. What did Elrond carry on his way to the Grey Havens?

# 50. ELVISH TOO

1. Quenya was the language spoken by the —— Elves.
2. Sindarin was the language of the —— elves.
3. Which of the above languages was an ancient tongue of Eldamar?
4. What was the High-elven name for all of the Elves, and what did it mean?
5. The words *"elda"* and *"edhel"* are related to each other, both meaning ——. Identify their respective languages.
6. Give the two Quenya words for "star."
7. How do you tell a horse to "giddap" in Elvish?
8. Give the Sindarin and Quenya names for the Moon.
9. What two parts of the body do the hill-names Amon Hen and Amon Lhaw allude to?
10. How do you request an Elvish ostler to "fill up my cup again"?

## 51. GANDALF

1. Describe Gandalf's physical appearance when he visited the Shire.
2. What was Gandalf best known for in the Shire?
3. What was Gandalf's name in the Elder Days, when he lived in Valinor, and what sort of being was he?
4. By whom was Gandalf called Mithrandir?
5. When did Gandalf reveal that he had been imprisoned by Saruman?
6. On Mount Caradhras, what did Gandalf do as he said "naur an edraith ammen!"?
7. Who were the first members of the Fellowship to hear the outcome of Gandalf's battle with the Balrog?
8. How did Gandalf determine that Bilbo's ring, taken from Gollum, was the One Ring?
9. What weapon did Gandalf carry after 2941 TA?
10. What were Gandalf's last words at the Grey Havens before setting sail from Middle-earth?

## 52. DRAGONS

1. Name the three breeds of dragons in Middle-earth.
2. Which dragon fell upon the towers of Thangorodrim?
3. Give the full name of the dragon in *Farmer Giles of Ham*.
4. What dragons lived in the Ered Mithrin mountains?
5. What parts of Scatha the Worm were sent to the Dwarves?
6. Why were Fingon's archers able to turn back Glaurung at Ard-galen?
7. How did Glaurung stop Túrin Turambar outside Nargothrond and cause Nienor to lose her memory?
8. What was Smaug's weakest spot as discovered by Bilbo?
9. Who confronted the winged dragons of Morgoth in the final battle of the Valar against Morgoth?
10. What was the name of the region in the eastern range of the Grey Mountains where dragons lived?

# 53. RINGS AND THINGS

1. How did Feänor make the Silmarils?
2. What ultimately became of the three Silmarils?
3. Name the chain wrought by Aulë to bind Melkor.
4. What necklace had five hundred emeralds as green as grass?
5. Translated from the Black Speech, what was written on the One Ring?
6. What was the Phial of Galadriel?
7. Give the Quenya names for the Ring of Fire, the Ring of Air, and the Ring of Water, and tell who wore them during the War of the Ring.
8. What were the *palantíri*?
9. Give the location of each of the seven Palantíri as they were distributed by Elendil in his realm.
10. What jewelry did Gandalf give Old Took?

# 54. ROHAN

1. Where was the Muster of Rohan held?
2. What was the Rohirrim name for Lórien, and what did it mean?
3. What king of Rohan was known as "The Old"?
4. *Rohirrim* means "Horse-lords" and is derived from the Sindarin word "*roch*," meaning "horse." What is the related Quenya word for "horse"?
5. What was an "*éored*"?
6. Where in Rohan was the hamlet of Upbourn?
7. Who was struck by King Helm's fist and died soon after?
8. What was the Sindarin name of the caves under Helm's Deep?
9. Name the minstrel of Théoden who wrote a song about Théoden's death.
10. What and where was Firienwood?

# 55. THE COURT OF THE STEWARD

1. Denethor II was what number in the line of the ruling Stewards of Gondor?
2. How were Boromir and Faramir related?
3. Why did Boromir come to Rivendell at the time of the Council of Elrond?
4. How did Denethor II come under the influence of Sauron?
5. To what temptation did Boromir yield?
6. Where did Frodo and Sam first meet Faramir?
7. Who was made a Guard of the Citadel by Denethor II?
8. When the wounded Faramir was brought back into Minas Tirith, what did Denethor order in his madness?
9. When Faramir surrendered the office of Steward to Aragorn, what was Aragorn's response?
10. Whom did Faramir marry?

# 56. SIGN ON THE DOTTED LINE

Match the character with his signature. Please keep in mind that a character may have more than one name.

1. Balin

a. [signature in Tengwar script]

2. Celebrimbor

b. [signature in Tengwar script]

3. Daeron

c. [signature in Tengwar script]

4. Fëanor

d.

[signature in Tengwar script]

5. Galadriel

e. [signature in Cirth runes]

6. Gandalf

f. [signature in Cirth runes]

7. Elrond

g. [signature in Cirth runes]

8. Sam

h. [signature in Tengwar script]

9. Aragorn

i. [signature in Tengwar script]

10. Uglúk

j. [signature in Tengwar script]

# 57. FRODO

1. How were Frodo and Bilbo related?
2. Where did Frodo say he was moving to when he sold Bag End?
3. When did Frodo disappear in the Inn of the Prancing Pony?
4. Who was the small dark figure that Frodo saw seated on a stool in Rivendell?
5. With what words did Frodo accept his mission to destroy the One Ring?
6. What did Frodo say to Gollum which proved to be a prophetic statement?
7. With what light did Frodo force Shelob to retreat?
8. While in Mordor, how did Frodo see the Ring in his mind?
9. Where did Frodo stay while Bagshot Row was being restored?
10. For whom did Frodo leave the last pages of the Red Book?

## 58. MERRY AND PIPPIN

1. Give Merry's full name.
2. What was the title of the book by Merry that discussed the relationship between Rohirric and Hobbitish?
3. To whom did Merry say, "As a father you shall be to me"?
4. Who approached Merry when he walked away from the Prancing Pony at night?
5. Who took Pippin to Minas Tirith?
6. Who was younger—Merry or Pippin?
7. What dangerous deed did Pippin do that revealed him to Sauron?
8. What act of bravery did Merry perform in the Battle of the Pelennor Fields?
9. Whom did the Rohirrim call Holdwine of the Shire—Merry or Pippin?
10. Where were Merry and Pippin buried?

## 59. GIMLI

1. How did Gimli happen to be present at the Council of Elrond?
2. What did Haldir tell Gimli when he removed the blindfold from his eyes?
3. What gift did Gimli ask of Galadriel?
4. When Gimli tried to attack Gandalf thinking he was Saruman, what happened to his ax?
5. How many Orcs did Gimli kill at the Battle of Helm's Deep?
6. What did Gimli hope to find in the ruins of Isengard?
7. What was it that Gimli noticed about Merry and Pippin as he saw them again at Isengard?
8. Where did Gimli settle after the War of the Ring?
9. What did he forge for Minas Tirith?
10. After the passing of Elessar, what did Gimli do?

## 60. FAMILY TREE

Match the closely related characters, then explain their exact family tie.

|   |   |   |   |
|---|---|---|---|
| 1. | Eärendil | a. | Merimas |
| 2. | Arwen | b. | Faramir |
| 3. | Glóredhel | c. | Lúthien |
| 4. | Belegund | d. | Morwen |
| 5. | Boromir | e. | Handir |
| 6. | Galadriel | f. | Caranthir |
| 7. | Dora | g. | Frodo |
| 8. | Gorbulas | h. | Elrond |
| 9. | Melian | i. | Idril |
| 10. | Fëanor | j. | Orodreth |

# 61. TREE FAMILY

1. Name the Two Trees of Valinor.
2. What color of light came from Telperion, and what color of light came from Laurelin?
3. On what mound in Valinor did the Two Trees grow?
4. Who killed the Two Trees?
5. What tree that did not give light of its own was given to the Elves in Tirion?
6. Name the White Tree that grew in Tol Eressëa.
7. What tree blossomed in the court of the king in Armenelos?
8. Give the plural form for the tree name "*mallorn*."
9. Name the trees after which the Field of Cormallen was named.
10. What happened to the Withered Tree of Minas Tirith after Aragorn and Gandalf brought in the new sapling?

# 62. TOM BOMBADIL

1. Give the first line of the song Tom Bombadil was singing when Frodo first heard his voice.
2. What was Tom carrying in his hands when the hobbits first caught sight of him?
3. From what dangerous situation did Tom rescue Merry?
4. How could Tom's manner of speech be described?
5. In the poem "The Adventures of Tom Bombadil," whose daughter was Goldberry?
6. When Frodo asked Goldberry who Tom was, what did she answer?
7. What was Tom Bombadil's Elvish name, and what did it mean?
8. When Tom put on the Ring, what failed to happen?
9. What did Tom tell the hobbits to do if they should fall into danger?
10. After he had rescued them from the mounds of the Barrow-wights, what did Tom tell the hobbits to do?

# 63. DO YOU UNDERSTAND ELVISH?

1. Who invented the oldest Eldarin letters?
2. Who remodeled and systematized these letters into the script used throughout the Third Age, and what was that script called?
3. What were the *tyeller*?
4. What is the name of the upside-down version of the letter named *parma*?
5. The Quenya word "formen," meaning north, refers literally to the —— -hand region.
6. What did the word "*periannath*" mean in Sindarin?
7. Give the Quenya name for the Children of Ilúvatar.
8. What was the Sindarin name for the Westron term "The Netted Stars"?
9. What was the name given to Men by the Eldar, and what did it mean?
10. Give both the Quenya and Sindarin forms of the word "winter."

# 64. LEGOLAS

1. What did the name *Legolas* mean in Sindarin?
2. Who was the father of Legolas, and what was he called in *The Hobbit*?
3. What was Legolas's weapon?
4. In what colors was Legolas dressed when the hobbits first saw him at Rivendell?
5. What bad tidings did Legolas bring to the Council of Elrond?
6. What was the lament of the Stones of Hollin that Legolas claimed he could hear?
7. What song did Legolas sing for the Fellowship in Lothlórien?
8. Upon what horse did Legolas ride with Gimli?
9. What did Legolas see flying inland over the River Anduin?
10. After the War of the Ring, what land did Legolas help beautify?

# 65. LOTHLÓRIEN

1. Lothlórien was named after what place in Valinor?
2. How did the Fellowship reach the court of Galadriel and Celeborn?
3. When Galadriel and Celeborn greeted the Fellowship, in what color were they dressed?
4. What did the color of Celeborn's hair have to do with a certain tree in Tol Eressëa?
5. Who were Galadriel's parents?
6. From whom did Galadriel learn much wisdom when she dwelt in Doriath?
7. Who was the one child of Galadriel and Celeborn, and whom did she marry?
8. What name was given to the Elves of Lothlórien, and what did it mean in Sindarin?
9. What was the Quenya form of Galadriel's name?
10. Name the area of Lothlórien, between the Anduin and the Celebrant, where the parting feast for the Fellowship was held.

## 66. POETS

Match the poems or songs with the characters who recited or sang them.

1. "Oliphaunt"                                       a. Gandalf
2. "The Words of Mal-                                b. Legolas
   beth the Seer"
3. "The Man in the
   Moon Stayed Up
   Too Late"                                         c. Beren
4. "In Dwimordene, in
   Lórien"                                           d. Bilbo
5. "The world was young,
   the mountains
   green"                                            e. Sam
6. "Eärendil was a mar-
   iner"                                             f. Galadriel
7. "In the Willow-meads
   of Tasarinan"
8. "The Song of Parting"                             g. Aragorn
9. "Silver flow the                                  h. Frodo
   streams from Celos
   to Erui"                                          i. Treebeard
10. "I sang of leaves, of
    leaves of gold, and
    leaves of gold there
    grew"                                            j. Gimli

# 67. EMBLEMS

Match the emblems and flags with the individuals, house, tribe, or country they represent.

1. An eight-rayed silver star
2. A white horse on a green field
3. A winged sun
4. Blue and silver
5. A white tree on a black field, a silver crown, and seven stars
6. A moon disfigured by a death's head
7. A white hand on a black field
8. An anvil and hammer, a crown, and seven stars
9. A harp and a torch
10. Gold and black

a. Saruman
b. House of Fingolfin
c. Ar-Pharazôn
e. Minas Morgul

e. Finwë
f. Rohan
g. Finrod Felagund
h. House of Fëanor
i. Elendil's heirs in Gondor
j. Durin

## 68. TOLKIEN QUERIES

1. Why did some of the Quendi hide when Oromë came?

2. What does the sequence *"min, ad, nel"* signify in Grey-elven?

3. Name the colors originally associated with Saruman, Gandalf, and Radagast.

4. True or false: Bilbo was Loblia's cousin.

5. What were backarappers, squibs, elf-fountains, and goblin barkers?

6. Name the kind of pipeweed that Butterbur gave Gandalf and the hobbits upon their return to Bree.

7. What does an innkeeper who has run out of wine containers have in common with a village in the Shire?

8. True or false: The "Bilbo's Last Song" poster was copyrighted by Tolkien.

9. Name two inanimate objects in Middle-earth that actually spoke.

10. What color was the flower *niphredil*?

# 69. SAURON

1. In the beginning, what was Sauron?
2. What was Sauron's name in Sindarin?
3. What fortress did Sauron command when he was the lieutenant of Melkor?
4. By what deceit did Sauron trap Gorlim?
5. How did Sauron come to Númenor?
6. What name did Sauron give himself when he visited the Elves in Eregion?
7. Where did Sauron forge the One Ring?
8. When did Sauron lose the power to appear fair to the eyes of Men?
9. Where did Sauron dwell when he was known as The Necromancer?
10. When the One Ring was cast into Orodruin, as what figure was Sauron last seen?

## 70. WHODUNITS

1. Who was changed into a great white bird?
2. Who had a special talent at the court of Arvedui?
3. Who warned Círdan of the peril of Nargothrond?
4. Who stood under the rain, arms raised?
5. Who counselled Isildur to cast the One Ring into Orodruin?
6. Who lived in Rivendell after the death of her husband in 2933 TA?
7. Who seemed as light as a feather with the sun shining through him?
8. Who were the nine members of the Fellowship?
9. Who were known to most people in Middle-earth as wizards?
10. Who used the leaves of kingsfoil for healing?

# 71. THE INKLINGS

1. Who were the Inklings?
2. Where did they meet on Tuesdays, and where did they meet on Thursdays?
3. What did the Inklings usually read to each other at these sessions?
4. Which of the following people were known to have attended Inkling meetings—Owen Barfield or George MacDonald?
5. Who was known as "Warnie"?
6. In what unfinished story did Tolkien use the Inklings as a setting?
7. Name a Dominican priest who often attended meetings of the Inklings.
8. What kind of novels did Charles Williams write?
9. While Williams enjoyed chapters from *The Lord of the Rings*, what did Tolkien think of Williams's novels?
10. Which name, from Tolkien's stories of Middle-earth, appeared misspelled in *That Hideous Strength* by C. S. Lewis?

# 72. BEREN AND LÚTHIEN

1. Through what land, where the sorcery of Sauron mingled with the magic of Melian, did Beren pass before he came to Doriath?
2. Lúthien's father was an Elf. What was her mother?
3. When Beren first saw Lúthien under the moonlight, what was she doing?
4. What name did Beren give Lúthien before he knew her real name, and what did it mean?
5. Which two sons of Fëanor captured Lúthien and which one fell in love with her?
6. What was Huan, the great hound from Valinor, able to do on only three occasions in his lifetime?
7. What did Beren, Lúthien, and Sauron have in common?
8. What did Beren and Lúthien take from Morgoth?
9. How did Beren come by the name Erchamion, which means "one-handed"?
10. Where did Lúthien go to seek Beren after his death?

## 73. "SMITH OF WOOTTON MAJOR"

1. What was the name of the apprentice brought to Wootton Major by one of the Master Cooks?
2. For what feast did the Master Cook make the Great Cake?
3. How did Smith receive the star?
4. How did the star get on Smith's forehead?
5. During one of Smith's journeys to Faery, how many mariners came out of a ship from the Sea of Windless Storm?
6. What was unusual about the leaves, flowers, and fruits of the King's Tree in Faery?
7. What did Smith keep in a casket that was eventually passed on as a family heirloom?
8. What message did the Queen of Faery ask Smith to convey to the King of Faery?
9. A Master Cook named Rider had put the star in a box in the kitchen storeroom. What was Rider's relationship to Smith?
10. What did Alf finally reveal to Nokes?

# 74. ARAGORN AND ARWEN

1. What was Aragorn named by Éomer?
2. Where did Aragorn and Arwen pledge their troth?
3. Whom did Aragorn find that Gandalf needed to question?
4. By what name did Aragorn first introduce himself to Frodo, Sam, and Pippin?
5. Whose daughter was Arwen?
6. When Aragorn was adopted by Elrond, what name was he given to hide his true identity, and what did it mean?
7. What did Galadriel give to Aragorn that had the same name as his kingly monicker?
8. On what day were Aragorn and Arwen wed?
9. In addition to a lifespan three times that of Men of Middle-earth, what else was granted to Aragorn?
10. After the death of Aragorn, where did Arwen go for her final resting place?

# 75. BLANKETY-BLANKS

1. Tolkien was a professor of —— at Merton College.
2. A Stone bridge, probably built by Dwarves, crossed the Esgalduin on the road from —— to ——.
3. "—— was a man who lived in the midmost part of the Island of Britain."
4. The sea of Helcar was located where formerly stood ——.
5. "I am the ——. I was chosen for the ——."
6. "This paperback edition, and no other, has been published with ——."
7. In Quenya, growing things with roots in the ground are called ——.
8. Bilbo thought of calling his memoirs *There and Back Again*, ——.
9. "Faithful servant yet master's bane, ——."
10. In *The Hobbit*, the Wood-elves who guarded the Dwarves fell asleep after drinking wine from the vintage of the gardens of ——.

# 76. DATE QUIZ

Match the date with the event.

1. 2899 SA

a. Ar-Adûnakhôr takes the sceptre of Númenor

2. February 15, 1934 AD

b. "The Adventures of Tom Bombadil" published in *The Oxford Magazine*

3. October 6, 1421 SR

c. Publication of "The Return of the King"

4. 1463 SR

d. Samwise returns to Bag End

5. 442 SA

e. End of the War of the Ring

6. December 23, 1937 AD

f. The Mallorn flowers in the Party Field

7. October 20, 1955 AD

g. Tolkien sees *Peter Pan* in a Birmingham theater

8. April 6, 1420 SR

h. North Polar Bear falls into the Christmas Tree

9. April, 1910 AD

i. Death of Elros Tar-Minyatur

10. November 3, 3019 TA

j. Faramir Took marries Goldilocks, daughter of Samwise

## 77. MELKOR/MORGOTH

1. When the Valar came down to Arda, what did Melkor do?
2. What was the name of the fortress that Melkor built under the Earth?
3. Which two Lamps built by the Valar to light Middle-earth did Melkor tear down?
4. Who wrestled with Melkor in the pits of Utumno?
5. For how long was Melkor imprisoned in the halls of Mandos?
6. What monster aided Melkor in the destruction of the Two Trees of Valinor?
7. Who named Melkor "Morgoth," meaning "the Black Foe of the World"?
8. What did Melkor do with the Silmarils after he stole them?
9. When Fingolfin challenged Morgoth to a duel, how did Morgoth appear to him?
10. Who was held captive for twenty-eight years atop Thangorodrim and forced to observe the world through the deceits of Morgoth?

## 78. ORCS

1. What Orc king had a well known game named after him as a result of his death?
2. Who were the Uruk-hai?
3. What was the insignia on the gear of Shagrat's company?
4. What did "*snaga*" mean in the Black Speech?
5. Who called the Orcs "*burárum*"?
6. Of what band of Orcs was Uglúk captain?
7. What was the Sindarin name for the Orcs?
8. From what creatures did Morgoth breed the Orcs?
9. Which Orc carried Merry and Pippin far enough for them to escape the attack of the Rohirrim?
10. What did the Orcs of Shagrat and those of Gorbag fight about?
11. Name the capital of the Orcs of the Misty Mountains.

# 79. SARUMAN

1. What was Saruman called by the Elves?
2. As the leader of the Istari, what was Saruman's color?
3. Who built the tower of Orthanc?
4. When did Saruman come to Isengard and start living in Orthanc?
5. What was in Orthanc which Saruman thought to use for his own devices but instead put him under Sauron's power?
6. Why did Saruman persuade the White Council not to drive Sauron out of Dol Guldur?
7. When Gandalf visited Saruman in Orthanc, what was peculiar about Saruman's robes?
8. Who surrounded Orthanc and imprisoned Saruman?
9. What was Saruman known as during the scouring of the Shire?
10. What happened immediately after Saruman fell dead?

# 80. TOWERS

1. In the First Age, the name Minas Tirith was given to the tower on Tol Sirion. Which character prominent in the Third Age dwelt for a time in that tower?
2. What was the White Tower?
3. In Sindarin the word "*minas*" means "tower." What other Sindarin word means "tower"?
4. Palantíri were kept in which of these towers: Amon Sûl, the Tower of Ingwë, the Tower of Cirith Ungol, or Annúminas?
5. What two towers were called the Teeth of Mordor?
6. Turgon fashioned two sculptures kept in the Tower of the King in Gondolin. What were they called?
7. What were the most unusual guards of the Tower of Cirith Ungol called?
8. Who built Minas Morgul, and what was its original name?
9. What was Orthanc made from?
10. In what tower was the chief *palantír* kept, and from what other tower could it be seen through another palantír?

# 81. QUOTE, UNQUOTE

Who said the following?

1. "Nasty, unhealthy parts, evidently. I shan't go any further this way tonight."
2. "All I knew was that you might be found in a wild region with the uncouth name of Shire."
3. "Who is the Lord of the Darkness?"
4. "There is nothing like looking if you want to find something."
5. "You will meet many foes, some open and some disguised; and you may find friends upon your way when you least look for it."
6. "May the stars shine upon your faces."
7. "Faithless is he that says farewell when the road darkens."
8. "Great kings may take what is their right."
9. "I feel as if I was *inside* a song, if you take my meaning."
10. "Don't Orcs eat, and don't they drink? Or do they just live on foul air and poison?"

## 82. WRITE IT RIGHT

Choose the more correct transcription for each name or phrase according to languages and associated modes, spelling, and so on.

1. *Ash nazg durbatulûk*   a.
   b.

2. *Lasselanta*   a.
   b.

3. Khazad-dûm   a.
   b.

4. Nargothrond   a.
   b.

5. John Ronald Reuel Tolkien   a.
   b.

6. *Et Eärello Endorenna utúlien*   a.
   b.

7. Karningul   a.
   b.

(Continued on page 84)

8. Ingwë a. *[tengwar script]*

b. *[tengwar script]*

9. Amon Lhaw a. *[tengwar script]*

b. *[tengwar script]*

10. abbreviation for "of
the" a. *[tengwar script]*

b. *[tengwar script]*

## 83. ELVES

1. Who was the Dark Elf of Nan Elmoth?
2. What was the birthname of Gil-galad, and what did it
mean in Sindarin?
3. Who were the Green Elves?
4. Who was Saeros?
5. What land was settled in 750 SA by the Gwaith-i-
Mírdain?
6. Who was the greatest jewel-smith of Eregion?
7. What was the name of the platforms built by the
Elves who lived in trees?
8. Who was the only woman to play a prominent part in
the debate of the Noldor about the theft of the Silmarils?
9. Which son of Fëanor was known as a mighty singer
whose voice was heard far over land and sea?
10. Which group of Elves built Alqualondë?

# 84. PUBLISHING TOLKIEN

1. In what year was *The Hobbit* first published in England by Allen & Unwin?
2. What edition of *The Hobbit* was published as a paperback in February, 1966?
3. In what years was *The Hobbit* published in Poland, Japan, France, and Argentina?
4. In what magazine and in what year was *The Adventures of Tom Bombadil* first published?
5. *The Fellowship of the Ring, The Two Towers, and The Return of the King* were published separately by Allen & Unwin. Give the year of publication for each.
6. How many times was *The Fellowship of the Ring* reprinted in England between 1954 and 1966?
7. In what year did Allen & Unwin publish a one-volume paperback edition of *The Lord of the Rings?*
8. Give the name of the American magazine that first published *Smith of Wootton Major* in December, 1967.
9. In what magazine and in what year was "Leaf By Niggle" first published?
10. Give the year of publication of the English edition and the American edition of *The Road Goes Ever On.*

# 85. TOLKIENISMS

1. Esgaroth was a_ a) jewel, b) weapon, c) mountain peak, d) city.
2. The Mugworts were a) trolls, b) insects, c) hobbits d) spiders.
3. Melilot was the name of a) a man of Dol Amroth, b) a river in Beleriand, c) a flower growing in the Old Forest, d) a member of a hobbit family.
4. Alcarinquë was a) one of Fëanor's sons, b) a Sindarin Elf, c) a star, d) a Numenórean city.
5. The name Calmatéma was given to a) an island off the Bay of Balar, b) a series of Elvish letters, c) a prince of the House of Elros, d) a mountain pass near Rohan.
6. The green mound before the western gate of Valimar was called a) Eryn Lasgalen, b) Esgalduin, c) Ezelbizar, d) Ezellohar.
7. One of the following names applies to someone rescued by Túrin Turambar: a) Dorlas, b) Guthláf, c) Echuir, d) Beleth.
8. One of the following words meant "singers" in Quenya: a) *Aelin*, b) *Lómelindi*, c) *Lindar*, d) *Linaewen*.
9. Lithlad was a) a calendar day in the Shire, b) a town in the Lebennin region of Gondor, c) a plain in Mordor, d) a minstrel from the court of Theoden.
10. Thargelion was formerly called a) Talath Dirnen, b) Teiglin, c)Talath Rhúnen, d) Thuringwethil.

# 86. THE CALENDAR OF THE ELDAR

1. The Quenya word for year was *"yén."* A *yén* would be equivalent to how many of our years?
2. When did the Elvish day begin and end?
3. What did the Elves use for ritual rather than practical purposes?
4. In Middle-earth, the Eldar observed a solar year. What were its two names?
5. Give the other name for the Calendar of Imladris.
6. What was the first day of the Elves' solar year?
7. How many seasons was this year divided into?
8. Give the translation for the seasons *lairë*, *quellë*, and *coirë*.
9. What season was also called *"Lasse-lanta,"* meaning "leaf-fall"?
10. What were the *enderi*?

# 37. "LEAF BY NIGGLE"

1. What picture was Niggle painting that was so large that he needed a ladder to work on it?
2. For whom did he do odd jobs, somewhat grudgingly?
3. Who called on Niggle after he recovered from his cold and was trying to get back to his painting?
4. After his train journey, why was Niggle sent to the Workhouse?
5. While Niggle was lying in the dark in the Workhouse infirmary, what did he hear?
6. What sounded to him like a summons to a King's feast?
7. Where did a second train ride take Niggle?
8. What caused him to fall off his bicycle?
9. What did schoolmaster Atkins find after Niggle's painting had been used to patch up Parish's roof?
10. What name was given to the area where Niggle found his tree, and where both he and Parish convalesced?

# 88. NÚMENOR: THE AKALLABÉTH

1. Who was the first ruling queen of Númenor?
2. To which of the Faithful of Númenor were the seven *palantíri* given?
3. Where on Númenor was the Hallow of Eru?
4. How many kings and queens ruled Númenor before the reign of Ar-Pharazôn?
5. Why did some of the Númenórean kings envy the Valar?
6. Into what two groups did the Númenóreans become divided?
7. Which Númenórean king forbade the use of the Elven-tongues?
8. What was the name of the daughter of Tar-Palantír, and what was it changed to when Ar-Pharazôn forced her to marry him?
9. On how many ships did Elendil's people set sail at the sinking of Númenor?
10. Who were the two sons of Elendil?

## 89. MAP READING

1. What two rivers joined to form the Gwathlo?
2. Name the seven beacon hills of Anórien, starting with the closest to Minas Tirith.
3. Where was the river Ringló, and of what other river was it a tributary?
4. Give the Khuzdul name for the Mirrormere.
5. What was the Elvish name for the Outer Sea encircling Arda?
6. Name a valley in Gondor noted for its roses.
7. What was the meaning of the name Tol Eressëa in Elvish?
8. What was the Thrihyrne?
9. Where was the Elvet-Isle?
10. Give the original name of Mirkwood.

# 90. SUMMA . . .

1. Who explained Tolkien's scholarly parodies in the poems of *"The Adventures of Tom Bombadil and Other Verses from the Red Book"*?
2. In what book about Tolkien was the "thoughtography" of Ted Serios explained?
3. The title of the book of essays *Tolkien and the Critics* is derived from the title of what lecture by Tolkien?
4. "Gollum's Character Transformation in *The Hobbit*," "Aspects of the Paradisiacal in Tolkien's Work," and "Everyclod and Everyhero: The Image of Man in Tolkien" are titles of essays from what book about Tolkien?
5. In 1966, what American scholar visited Tolkien to help him work on *The Silmarillion?*
6. From whose book are these chapters: "Middle-earth: an Imaginary World?" and "Sauron and the Nature of Evil"?
7. Both *The Complete Guide to Middle-earth* and *The Tolkien Companion* are great aids to Tolkien fans. Who are the authors?
8. In 1958, to what American university did Tolkien sell the manuscripts of *The Hobbit* and *The Lord of the Rings?*
9. For what series of books did Robley Evans write *J. R. R. Tolkien?*
10. What degree did Tolkien receive from Oxford University for his contribution to philology?

1. Who wrote: "This book, with the help of maps, does not need any illustrations, it is good and should appeal to all children between the ages of five and nine"?
2. When *The Fellowship of the Ring* was first published, who opened his review with, "This book is like lightning from a clear sky"?
3. From what newspaper is this quote: "A wonderful story, set in a world which paralyzes the imagination, and told in magnificent prose"?
4. What did *The Spectator* reviewer say of *The Return of the King*?
5. Who looked for *The Lord of the Rings* for four years after reading W. H. Auden's review in *The New York Times*?
6. What famous actor said, "I consider, and have considered for some years, that Tolkien is one of the great writers of our time"?
7. What other books did *The Lord of the Rings* replace as a bestseller on American campuses in the mid-sixties?
8. Which well-known contemporary author entitled his review of *The Silmarillion*, "The Prince of Fantasists, J. R. R. Tolkien"?
9. Who wrote, in a review of *The Silmarillion*, ". . . Tolkien's vision is philosophically and morally powerful . . ."?
10. What gave *Los Angeles Times* reviewer Robert Kirsch a better understanding of *The Silmarillion*?

# 92. IN PARTICULAR

1. How did the opening sentence of *The Hobbit* originate?
2. What were Belthil and Glingal?
3. Name the source of the dark Flame of the Balrogs.
4. In his description of hobbits in *The Hobbit*, what did Tolkien write about their fingers?
5. What was the Sindarin name for the Barrow-downs?
6. Who was known as the Flammifer of Westernesse?
7. What food did hobbits have a passion for?
8. Give the more familiar name for the Hithaeglir.
9. Who was the grandfather of Bergil, a man of Gondor?
10. What ended with the second mingling of the lights of Telperion and Laurelin?

## 93. THE DWARVISH LANGUAGE

Match the Dwarvish names with the places to which they refer.

1. Barazinbar
2. Kheled-zâram
3. Gabilgathol
4. Zirak-zigil
5. Tumunzahar
6. Bundushathûr
7. Azanulbizar
8. Khazad-dûm
9. Nulukkizdîn

a. Celebdil
b. Nogrod
c. Mirrormere
d. Moria
e. Nargothrond
f. Caradhras
g. Fanuidhol
h. Nanduhirion
i. Belegost

# 94. "THE FATHER CHRISTMAS LETTERS"

1. When did Father Christmas send his first letter to John Tolkien?
2. What was written on the envelope sent by Father Christmas in 1932?
3. What year did the North Polar Bear fall down the main stairs?
4. Who fought the Goblins during their November, 1933, attack and enjoyed it immensely?
5. In 1935, who turned everything into a game while helping Father Christmas?
6. What character in *The Father Christmas Letters* has a name almost the same as an important character in *The Silmarillion*?
7. What happened to the North Pole in 1925?
8. In 1937, because Father Christmas was unable to write to the Tolkien children, his secretary wrote instead. What did the secretary write at the end of the letter?
9. In answer to the requests of the Tolkien children, what did the North Polar Bear send them?
10. When did Father Christmas plant a Christmas tree from Norway in a pool of ice at the North Pole?

# 95. TOLKIEN TALKING

1. In the record album, *Poems and Songs of Middle-earth*, which poems does Tolkien read on bands two and four of side one?
2. In this same album, who sings "The Road Goes Ever On" song cycle?
3. Who composed the music for "The Road Goes Ever On," and what musical revue had he previously been noted for?
4. Who made the tape recordings used for the two albums in which Tolkien read and sang from *The Hobbit* and *The Lord of the Rings*?
5. Before reading from his own books, what did Tolkien recite on the tape recorder?
6. On which tracks of which albums are these lines read: "Treebeard fell silent," "When evening in the Shire," "Hey! Come merry doll!," "A little way back"?
7. In the second album, on which track does Tolkien chant "Namarië" in Elvish?
8. When were these tape recordings made?
9. Who wrote some notes on Tolkien and his books for the back cover of *Poems and Songs of Middle-earth*?
10. What story from *The Silmarillion* has Christopher Tolkien recorded?

# 96. THE COURT OF ROHAN

1. With whom did Éomer and Théoden strike up a bargain to lead the Rohirrim through Druadan Forest?
2. Who was the Father of Gríma?
3. To which line of the kings of Rohan did Théoden belong?
4. Who healed Théoden from the despair caused by the spells of Saruman?
5. Who was in Théoden's disfavor because of Gríma Wormtongue's plots?
6. Who was Théodred, and in what battle was he killed?
7. How did Éowyn manage to take part in the Battle of The Pelennor Fields?
8. How did Aragorn heal Éowyn from the effects of the Black Breath?
9. How did King Théoden die?
10. What did Grima Wormtongue do after Saruman was banished from Isengard?

# 97. TOLKIEN FANDOM

1. In 1965, during the popularity of the paperback editions of Tolkien's books, who founded The Tolkien Society of America?
2. What inspired him to seek out other Tolkien fans?
3. What happened as a result of the popularity of the Tolkien Society?
4. Name at least two Tolkien buttons popular in the sixties.
5. In Los Angeles, a group of Tolkien fans who had read the hardcover edition of *The Lord of the Rings* formed a group which preceded the Tolkien Society by five years. What was it called?
6. What hobbit custom was adopted by Tolkien fans at Bilbo and Frodo Birthday picnics?
7. What strange game became a tradition at these gatherings?
8. For practical reasons, issues of the Tolkien Society's *Tolkien Journal* were combined with which of these publications from other groups: *I Palantír, Orcrist, Entmoot*, or *Mythlore*?
9. What became of the Tolkien Society of America?
10. When and by whom was the British Tolkien Society founded?

## 98. TENGWAR MATCH

Match the Elvish characters with their Quenya names.

1. ɱ                a. *thúle*

2. ρ                b. *vilya*

3. ɋ                c. *ungwe*

4. ↄl                d. *anca*

5. ᴜ                e. *halla*

6. o                f. *parma*

7. ȝ                g. *alda*

8. ʕ                h. *númen*

9. |                i. *áre* (or *esse*) *nuquerna*

10. þ                j. *úre*

# 99. THE NÚMENÓREAN CALENDAR

1. Name the leap year of the Númenórean calendar, and give its meaning in Quenya.
2. How was this leap year lengthened?
3. What was the calendar system of Númenor called in Arnor and Gondor?
4. Give the name of the fourth day of the Númenórean week named in honor of the White Tree.
5. When did the Númenórean calendar year begin?
6. What were the names of the second and third months, and what did they mean?
7. Name the month of the Númenórean year named after one of the Valár.
8. What was the Elvish word for "month"?
9. Give the names for the month of flowering and for the month of cold.
10. Which three days did not belong in any month?

# 100. WRAP-UP

1. In what region of Middle-earth did Radagast live?
2. What was Pipeweed called in Gondor?
3. Who was the chieftain of the Woses?
4. In *The Hobbit*, what color stockings did Thorin wear?
5. What was the "Ring of Doom" called in Quenya?
6. Whose brother was the Silvan Elf Orophin?
7. What important scholarly book was written by Bilbo?
8. Name the son of Hildibrand Took.
9. What necklace was given to Finrod by the Dwarves of the Blue Mountains?
10. How many ponies did Tom Bombadil bring for the hobbits?
11. In what kind of ship did Galadriel and Celeborn sail to the farewell feast for the Fellowship?

# ANSWERS

## QUIZ 1

1. He was the first hobbit to cultivate pipe-weed
2. Hobbits of the Fourth Age descended from Sam Gamgee. They were the wardens of Westmarch.
3. Yellow and green
4. The down that many grew on their chins
5. Gollum
6. A collection of two-room dwellings
7. The hobbit brothers who founded the Shire
8. The Harfoots
9. *Banakil*, meaning "halfling"
10. The Mayor of Michel Delving who also served as Postmaster and First Shirriff

## QUIZ 2

1. A stone on the Great East Road which marked the center of the Shire
2. "The Floating Log" in Frogmorton; "Golden Perch" in Stock; "The Green Dragon" in Bywater; "The Ivy Bush" on Bywater Road
3. Bamfurlong
4. Mushrooms
5. Michel Delving
6. In the Brokenbores
7. Forty by fifty leagues
8. It had round windows and round doors
9. The second of November
10. Gorhendad Oldbuck

## QUIZ 3

1. *Lúmenn'*
2. *Yulma*
3. *Elye*
4. *Lómë*
5. *Hildinyar*
6. *Vedui*
7. *Ennorath*
8. *Firn*
9. *Teithant*
10. *Estel*

## QUIZ 4

1. Those on the left of the entrance hall
2. Approximately fifty years old
3. He started reading his morning mail
4. A mark that identified Bilbo as a burglar
5. Wednesday
6. Dwalin, Balin, Kíli, Fíli, Dori, Nori, Óri, Oin, Glóin, Bifur, Bofur, Bombur, and Thorin
7. Throng
8. Thorin
9. Bifur
10. Kíli and Fíli; Dori, Nori, and Óri; Bombur; Bifur and Bofur; Dwalin and Balin; and Thorin, respectively

## QUIZ 5

1. "Escaping goblins to be caught by wolves"
2. Roäc, chief of the great ravens of Erebor
3. Hundreds of butterflies
4. Wine
5. Bilbo was the lucky number
6. Smaug the Chiefest and Greatest of Calamities; Smaug the Mighty, and Lord Smaug the Impenetrable
7. Beorn
8. A necklace of silver and pearls given to him by Dáin
9. His belongings were being sold at auction
10. Balin


## QUIZ 6

1. Gollum
2. Teeth
3. The sun
4. A stool
5. "Handses"
6. "A box without hinges, key, or lid. Yet golden treasure inside is hid."
7. Time
8. "Give me more time!"
9. His "precious ring"
10. The sixth passage on the left

## QUIZ 7

1. That Aulë cause them to sleep until after the awakening of the Elves
2. Orfalch Echor
3. Minas Tirith
4. The treasures of the Dwarf-kings
5. Lefnui, Morthond, Ciril, Ringló, Gilrain, Serni, and Anduin
6. Valacirca
7. Treebeard
8. Three were recovered by Sauron and four were consumed by dragons
9. The *palantíri*, seeing stones made by Fëanor in Aman
10. The Chamber of Mazarbul


## QUIZ 8

1. He was a hobbit
2. Sméagol (or Trahald)
3. His friend Déagol
4. He claimed it was given to him as a birthday present by his grandmother
5. Goblin
6. Six
7. On an island in the middle of an underground lake
8. Yellow Face
9. "I will serve the master of the Precious."
10. "Precious!"

## QUIZ 9

1. i
2. g
3. j
4. b
5. h
6. f
7. c
8. e
9. a
10. d

## QUIZ 10

1. The cats of Queen Béruthiel
2. The horse of Eorl and the First of the Mearas
3. Insects in Bilbo's poem "Errantry"
4. Landroval
5. Snowmane, who fell on King Théoden
6. The thrushes and ravens
7. Grip, Fang, and Wolf
8. He was the chief of the great ravens of Erebor
9. The Great Boar of Everholt
10. Sharp-Ears, Wise Nose, Swish-tail, and Bumpkin

## QUIZ 11

1. g
2. f
3. h
4. j
5. a
6. c
7. b
8. i
9. d
10. e

## QUIZ 12

1. Opening; treachery
2. The harpers sadly sing
3. Nan-tasarion
4. Rippling streams; Water Hot; smokes and steams
5. Arvernien; Nimbrethil
6. *Carnimírië*; white the blossom lay
7. Let them pass; Let them pass; Pass them by; Pass them by
8. *Silivren*; *menel aglar*
9. Beware of the sea
10. Leaves of years; ray of star

## QUIZ 13

1. Farmer Maggot
2. Bullroarer Took; he knocked off the head of the Orc king with a wooden club
3. The fact that some of their members went on adventures
4. Messrs. Grubb, Grubb, and Burrowes
5. The Gamwiches, the Gammidges, and the Ropers
6. Hugo Bracegirdle, a hobbit who borrowed books but seldom returned them
7. Robin Smallburrow; the hobbit of Hobbiton who became a shiriff under Lotho Sackville-Baggins
8. A surname used by hobbits of Bree
9. *Ranugad*
10. Budgeford in Bridgefields


## QUIZ 14

1. John (1917), Michael (1920), Christopher (1924), and Priscilla (1929)
2. *The Homecoming of Beorhtnoth, Beorhthelm's Son*
3. A former student of Tolkien's who read the typescript of *The Hobbit* in 1936 and recommended it to a friend who worked for the publishers Allen & Unwin
4. Beren and Lúthien
5. 1931, 1930, 1926, and 1928, respectively
6. *The Lord of the Rings*
7. He was reciting Beowulf in Anglo-Saxon to his students
8. The Black Ogre
9. Gondolin and the Vale of Tumladen, Taniquetil, Nargothrond, and Tol Sirion, respectively
10. "The Road Goes Ever On" song cycle

## QUIZ 15

1. Samwise Gamgee (Banazîr Galpsi in Westron)
2. Gardening
3. At Number 3 Bagshot Row
4. Gandalf chose him to go with Frodo after he caught Sam eavesdropping
5. Elves
6. Slinker or Stinker (depending on Gollum's mood)
7. He decided to take the Ring and continue Frodo's mission
8. Because the Orcs who guarded Frodo fought and killed each other for Frodo's coat of Mithril-mail
9. Rose Cotton
10. Seven times

## QUIZ 16

1. Fangorn (Treebeard), Finglas (Leaflock), and Fladrif (Skinbark)
2. Fimbrethil, Fangorn's Entwife
3. Bregalad; he was a bit hastier than other Ents
4. Angrenost
5. C. S. Lewis
6. Onodrim
7. The Elves, The Dwarves, the Ents, and Men
8. Laurelindórenan
9. One glowed with golden light, the other with green
10. They disappeared after their land was ravaged by war and were lost to the Ents

## QUIZ 17

1. Eru
2. Angelic beings, the offspring of the thought of Ilúvatar
3. A vision of the world they had created with their song
4. Melkor
5. *Valar*; the Powers of the World
6. The radiant and majestic bodies in which the Valar appeared to Elves and Men
7. The Elves, who were the Firstborn, and Men, who were the Followers
8. To have them as subjects and servants and to be called Lord
9. The Imperishable Flame
10. Manwë


## QUIZ 18

1. The Lieutenant of the Dark Tower (Barad-dûr); "The Mouth of Sauron"
2. The Lord of the Nazgûl
3. A steel crown set on an invisible head with just fiery eyes shining above the shoulders
4. Nine
5. The Lieutenant of Minas Morgul
6. Black Speech; "ringwraith"
7. The Nazgûl, the Olog-hai, and other close servants of Sauron
8. Savage men from the land of Harad, south of Gondor
9. The Lord of the Nazgûl, when he reigned in Angmar
10. Angamaitë and Sangahyando

## QUIZ 19

1. In a lake near the West-gate of Moria
2. Gothmog
3. Sentient stone figures with three joined bodies, three vulture-like faces facing outward, inward, and across the gate, and with large clawlike hands upon their knees
4. When controlled by Sauron they could withstand sunlight
5. An evil spirit who was shaped as a monstrous spider
6. Light
7. Carcharoth
8. Fastitocalon
9. Shelob, the great spider
10. A large, dark manlike form with a fiery mane

## QUIZ 20

1. Elenna
2. From the Barrow Downs, through the Old Forest, and into the Brandywine at the southern end of Buckland
3. The burial mounds for both the Dúnedain and Rohirrim after the Battle of Pelennor Fields
4. The City of the Trees in Lothlórien, site of the court of Celeborn and Galadriel
5. A range of fertile green hills in the Anfalas coastal strip of Gondor (a/k/a The Green Ridges)
6. The Ered Nimrais, the White Mountains
7. The High Hay
8. Ascar, Thalos, Legolin, Brilthor, Duilwen, and Adurant
9. The caves in Aman where Ar-Pharazôn and his warriors were buried when they invaded the undying lands
10. The Cape of Forochel, inhabited by the Lossoth

## QUIZ 21

1. g, A
2. i, D
3. h, G
4. e, C
5. c, H
6. a, E
7. j, J
8. b, B
9. f, F
10. d, I

## QUIZ 22

1. Eagles
2. Ever
3. Peak
4. Series
5. Father
6. Fire
7. Foot
8. Ford
9. Iron
10. Ships

## QUIZ 23

1. Afteryule, Solmath, Rethe, Astron, Thrimidge, Forel- ithe, Afterlithe, Wedmath, Halimath, Winterfilth, Blotmath, and Foreyule
2. The week
3. Saturday
4. Winterfilth
5. Solmath, Rethe, Thrimidge, and Wedmath
6. By ten days
7. Sterday, Sunday, Monday, Trewsday, Hevensday, Mersday, and Highday
8. Highday, corresponding to our Friday
9. Yuledays and Lithedays
10. "On Friday the first of summer-filth"


## QUIZ 24

7. Anglachel and Anguirel, forged by Eöl
2. The spear of Gil-Galad; in Sindarin, it meant "point white as snow"
3. Herugrim
4. Telchar, a Dwarf of Nogrod in the First Age
5. The first was Morgoth's mace; the second was a one hundred-foot battering ram made in Mordor to break the Gate of Minas Tirith
6. Farmer Giles of Ham
7. Thingol
8. The swords Orcrist and Glamdring
9. It was the great bow of Beleg
10. The Balrog

## QUIZ 25

1. *The Downfall of the Lord of the Rings and the Return of the King*
2. The journey of the Eldar, the three kindreds of Elves who traveled west across Middle-earth in the First Age
3. Elros and Elrond, the "half-elven" (*Peredhil*), the sons of Eärendil and Elwing; they were given the choice of belonging either to the race of Elves or the race of Men
4. The Red Book of the Periannath
5. One of the three trolls in *The Hobbit*
6. The name for the eleventh month of the year in Bree
7. The North Polar Bear's nephews in *The Father Christmas Letters*; Paksu means fat, Valkotukka means white hair
8. Elrond
9. By swans
10. Golasgil

## QUIZ 26

1. In Osgiliath
2. Ost-in-Edhil
3. Merethrond
4. The Chamber of Mazarbul
5. Three
6. Rómendacil II
7. Armenelos, a temple built by Sauron in Númenor
8. A spiral staircase in Khazad-dûm that went from the lowest dungeon to Durin's tower
9. The underground fortress of Nargothrond
10. In Rivendell

## QUIZ 27

1. Ostoher, Seventh King of Gondor
2. Barahir; he wrote the full tale of Aragorn and Arwen
3. The expansion of Gondor southward and westward through her fleets
4. When no claimant to the crown could be found after the disappearance of Eärnur
5. The heir of Isildur
6. Findegil, king's writer, who finished the most important copy of the Red Book
7. Osgiliath
8. When Minas Anor became the capital of Gondor
9. Dol Amroth
10. Belegorn

## QUIZ 28

1. Ægidius Ahenobarbus Julius Agricola de Hammo
2. "What is a blunderbuss?"
3. Old nails, bits of wire, pieces of broken pot, bones, and stones
4. "Help! help! help!"
5. Caudimordax
6. A Dragon's Tail, replaced by a Mock Dragon's Tail Cake
7. That he would pay for damages with all his treasure
8. "It's cruel hard!"
9. The dragon
10. Getting 'round his queen, Agatha

## QUIZ 29

1. Eärendil, the Mariner
2. Finduilas, wife of Denethor
3. The Dwarf king, Dáin Ironfoot
4. Gandalf
5. Sancho Proudfoot
6. Glorfindel
7. The Man in the Moon
8. Déagol, Gollum's cousin
9. Maglor, one of the two remaining sons of Fëanor
10. Galdor

## QUIZ 30

1. False; he was a Vala, usually named Mandos
2. True
3. True
4. False; he was a man of Gondor
5. False; it was an island
6. True
7. True
8. False; Nokes is the Master Cook in *Smith of Wootton Major*
9. True
10. False; in addition to runes, there were seven stars between a crescent moon and a rayed sun

## QUIZ 31

1. c
2. e
3. f
4. b
5. j
6. h
7. a
8. g
9. i
10. d

## QUIZ 32

1. Ragnor; not a hobbit
2. Eärendur; not an Elf
3. Astaldo; not a man
4. Eonwë; not a Vala
5. Forn; not a dwarf
6. Bregalad; not a beast
7. Blotmath; not an inanimate object
8. Gorbulas; not an Orc
9. *Elenya*; not a plant or tree
10. Garm; not from the tales of Middle-earth

## QUIZ 33

1. The name Bolger: Ray Bolger played the Scarecrow in *The Wizard of Oz*, and there was a family of hobbits called Bolger
2. A basket for seed is called a hobbet, or hobbit
3. The name of the goddess Kali is the same as the abbreviation of Kalimac, Merry's real Hobbitish name
4. Because in Westron Kali means "jolly and gay," whereas Kali is the goddess of Death
5. It was the piano upon which Donald Swann composed the music to the first six songs in "The Road Goes Ever On"
6. Yale; Yale was also a lowland area in the Eastfarthing of the Shire
7. Thúle; it is the name of tengwar number nine
8. The island of Malta; the Quenya word for gold is *malta*
9. *The Dark Tower*
10. Largo

## QUIZ 34

1. Azog; *The Return of the King*
2. Treebeard; *The Return of the King*
3. Gandalf; *The Two Towers*
4. The chief of the Lossoth (Snowmen of Forochel); *The Return of the King*
5. The Second Voice in "Leaf By Niggle;" *Tree and Leaf*
6. The King in "Farmer Giles of Ham"; *Smith of Wootton Major* and *Farmer Giles of Ham*
7. Strider; *Fellowship of the Ring*
8. C. S. Lewis; Tolkien biography by Carpenter
9. The purse of one of the trolls; *The Hobbit*
10. Mablung, a Ranger of Ithilien; *The Two Towers*

## QUIZ 35

1. c
2. d
3. a
4. g
5. b
6. h
7. j
8. e
9. i
10. f

## QUIZ 36

1. In *Smith of Wootton Major*
2. Narmacil and Minalcar
3. Because it was the gorge into which Nienor leaped to her death
4. The ruinous Fifth Battle of the Wars of Beleriand; meaning "Tears Unnumbered"
5. A sea monster, the last of the old Turtle-fish
6. A man of Bree, keeper of the western gate
7. Seven years
8. *The Homecoming of Beorhtnoth, Beorhthelm's Son;* Tidwald and Torthelm
9. A village in the Eastfarthing of the Shire
10. Gandalf, Radagast, and Saruman

## QUIZ 37

1. a
2. b
3. d
4. b
5. b
6. c
7. b
8. a
9. d
10. c

## QUIZ 38

1. John Ronald Reuel
2. Because of his daring unofficial raid against the Turks at the siege of Vienna in 1529, George Von Hohenzollern was given the nickname Tollkühn, meaning "foolhardy"
3. January 3, 1892, in Bloemfontein, Orange Free State, South Africa
4. A black servant of the Tolkien family who once "borrowed" J. R. R. to show his people a white baby
5. Tea Club, Barovian Society, a social group Tolkien belonged to when he was nineteen
6. Hilary
7. A dog owned by Father Francis Morgan, kept at Rednal where Mabel Tolkien and her boys stayed in 1904
8. He saw Welsh names on coal trucks
9. Nevbosh
10. Breakfast, practical joke, Martyr's Memorial, the Union

## QUIZ 39

1. Joseph Wright
2. By speaking fluent Gothic in his role as a barbarian envoy
3. Sugar cubes
4. She gave him a pen; he gave her a ten and six-penny watch
5. Edith singing and dancing in a wood near Roos, in 1917
6. Thirty-two
7. "The Bird and the Baby" was the nickname given to the Eagle and Child, an Oxford pub frequented by Tolkien and his friends, the Inklings
8. The cutting of branches from his neighbor's poplar tree
9. *Leaf by Niggle* and *Smith of Wootton Major*
10. The Miramar Hotel, Bournemouth

## QUIZ 40

1. d
2. h
3. j
4. b
5. g
6. i
7. a
8. f
9. e
10. c

## QUIZ 41

1. Dior and his descendants
2. The three mariners who reached Aman with Eärendil
3. Gimli, because he carried a lock of Galadriel's hair
4. The dwelling of Radagast the Brown
5. Henneth Annûn
6. The Sindarin name for Mount Everwhite
7. A village of Bree-land
8. Elwing, daughter of Dior and Nimloth, who was born on a night when the light of stars glittered in the spray of a waterfall
9. Eldacar
10. Grimbeorn

## QUIZ 42

1. c
2. e
3. h
4. d
5. f
6. a
7. i
8. g
9. j
10. b

## QUIZ 43

1. Milton Glaser
2. "Bilbo Comes to the Huts of the Raft-elves," "The Hill: Hobbiton-Across-the-Water," "Fangorn Forest," and "Barad-dûr," respectively
3. Pauline Baynes
4. Emus
5. Gandalf, a Nazgûl, and Sauron, respectively
6. The American edition features a photograph; the British version has a Pauline Baynes illustration
7. The front cover shows the Shire; the back cover shows Mount Doom; Pauline Baynes
8. Fëanor, Idril Celebrindal, Lúthien Tinúviel, Fingolfin, Elwë, and Finwë


## QUIZ 44

1. g, B
2. e, A; k, B
3. b, D
4. f, B
5. l, C
6. m, D
7. g, C
8. h, C; a, B
9. c, B
10. n, C
11. d, B
12. i, B

## QUIZ 45

1. False; not a Tolkien character
2. True
3. False; it was originally built by men of Gondor and called Minas Ithil
4. True
5. True
6. False; it was sung by Legolas
7. True
8. True
9. False; she was his eldest daughter
10. False; they were cousins


## QUIZ 46

1. Balbo Baggins
2. Daisy Gamgee; named after Sam's eldest sister
3. Frodo Gardner, first son of Sam and Rosie
4. Donnamira
5. Elfstan; meaning "elfstone"
6. Insengrim II
7. Saradoc Brandybuck
8. Tanta Hornblower
9. "The greenhanded" (Greenhand)
10. Hildifons and Isengar

## QUIZ 47

1. Bungo Baggins and Beladonna Took
2. A desire for adventures
3. Merry People
4. Ninety-nine
5. He put on the Ring and vanished
6. In an envelope on the mantelpiece
7. "... and he lived happily ever after to the end of his days"
8. Rivendell
9. As a small wrinkled creature with a hungry face
10. 131 years and eight days old

## QUIZ 48

1. Bifur, Bofur, and Bombur
2. Dis
3. Durin's Folk
4. Mahal, their name for Aulë
5. Daeron, minstrel and loremaster of King Thingol
6. Khuzdul, invented by Aulë
7. Barazinbar, Bundushathûr, and Zirak-zigil
8. Durin's Day
9. Noegyth Nibin
10. They shrank back from Aulë's hammer

## QUIZ 49

1. As the herald of Gil-galad
2. *Peredhil*, meaning "half-elven"
3. Imladris
4. Valandil
5. Erestor
6. *Miruvor*
7. The Ring of Barahir
8. Celebrian, daughter of Celeborn and Galadriel; El-
   ladan, Elrohir, and Arwen
9. Gandalf spoke the inscription of the One Ring in the
   Black Speech
10. A silver harp

## QUIZ 50

1. High
2. Grey
3. Quenya
4. Quendi; "the speakers, those that speak with voices"
5. Elf; *elda* is Quenya, *edhel* is Sindarin
6. *Elen, tinwë*
7. "*Noro lim!*"
8. Sindarin: Ithil; Quenya: Isil
9. Eye and ear
10. "*Enquanta nin i yulma*"

## QUIZ 51

1. An old man with a white beard hanging below his waist, wearing a long gray cloak, a silver scarf, a tall pointed blue hat and long black boots, and carrying a staff
2. His fireworks
3. Olórin; a Maia
4. By the Elves
5. At the Council of Elrond
6. He thrust the end of his staff into a piece of wood and set it aflame
7. Aragorn, Legolas, and Gimli
8. By casting it into the fireplace and seeing the inscription in fire-writing
9. The sword Glamdring
10. "I will not say: do not weep; for not all tears are an evil."

## QUIZ 52

1. The Urulóki, the Winged Dragons and the Cold-Drakes
2. Ancagalon the Black
3. Chrysophylax Dives
4. The Cold-Drakes
5. His teeth
6. Because he had not yet grown his full armor
7. By the spell of his eyes
8. A bare spot in his armor in the hollow of his left breast
9. Eärendil in his flying ship and all the great birds
10. Withered Heath

## QUIZ 53

1. He encased the blended light of the Two Trees of Valinor in three great jewels made of a special crystalline substance which he called silima
2. One was set on Eärendil's brow to sail with him across the sky, the second fell with Maedhros when he cast himself into a fiery abyss, and the third Maglor cast into the sea
3. Angainor
4. The necklace of King Girion
5. "One Ring to rule them all, One Ring to find them, One Ring to bring them all and in the darkness bind them"
6. A crystal jar containing the reflected light of Eärendil
7. Narya, worn by Gandalf; Vilya, worn by Elrond; and Nenya, worn by Galadriel
8. Crystal globes that showed scenes from faraway in space and time
9. The Dome of Stars in Osgiliath, Minas Ithil, Minas Anor, Orthanc, Annúminas, Elostirion in the Tower Hills, and the Tower of Amon Sûl
10. Magic diamond studs that fastened themselves and never came undone until ordered


## QUIZ 54

1. In the Valley of Harrowdale
2. Dwimordene, meaning "haunted valley"
3. Aldor
4. *Rokko*
5. A fighting unit of the army of Rohan
6. On the road between Dunharrow and Edoras
7. Freca
8. Aglarond, meaning "glittering caves"
9. Gléowine
10. An oak-wood on the border of Rohan and Gondor

1. Twenty-sixth
2. They were brothers, the sons of Denethor II
3. To find the answer to a dream he and his brother had had.
4. By looking into the *palantír* of Minas Tirith
5. He tried to take the Ring away from Frodo
6. In Henneth Annûn, the refuge of the Rangers of Ithilien
7. Pippin
8. That Faramir's body should be cremated
9. That the office of Steward should continue
10. Éowyn

**QUIZ 56**

1. f
2. d
3. e
4. c
5. j
6. i
7. b
8. h
9. a
10. g

## QUIZ 57

1. They were first *and* second cousins
2. Buckland
3. After jumping during a song and falling off a table
4. Bilbo
5. "I will take the Ring, though I do not know the way"
6. "If you touch me again, you shall be cast yourself into the Fire of Doom"
7. With the light from the Phial of Galadriel
8. As a great wheel of fire
9. At Farmer Cotton's
10. Sam


## QUIZ 58

1. Meriadoc Brandybuck (Kalimac Brandagamba in Westron)
2. *Old Words and Names in the Shire*
3. Théoden
4. Two Dark Riders
5. Gandalf
6. Pippin
7. He looked into the *palantír* of Orthanc
8. He helped Éowyn slay the Lord of the Nazgûl
9. Merry
10. In the House of the Kings in Gondor

## QUIZ 59

1. He had accompanied his father, Glóin, seeking advice from Elrond
2. That he was the first dwarf to behold the trees of Lórien since Durin's Day
3. A strand of her golden hair
4. It leapt from his hand and fell to the ground
5. Forty-two
6. Pipe-weed
7. That they had grown
8. In Aglarond, the glittering caves of Helm's Deep
9. New gates of mithril and steel
10. He sailed west over the Sea with Legolas

## QUIZ 60

1. i, son
2. h, daughter
3. e, mother
4. d, uncle
5. b, brother
6. j, sister
7. g, aunt
8. a, grandfather
9. c, mother
10. f, father

## QUIZ 61

1. Telperion and Laurelin
2. Silver light from Telperion; golden light from Laurelin
3. Ezellohar or Corollairë
4. Melkor and Ungoliant
5. Galathilion
6. Celeborn
7. Nimloth
8. *Mellyrn*
9. Culumalda trees
10. It was uprooted and laid to rest in Rath Dínen

## QUIZ 62

1. "Hey dol! merry dol! ring a dong dillo!"
2. A pile of white water lilies on a large leaf
3. He had been trapped by Old Man Willow
4. Singsongish
5. The River-woman
6. "He is"
7. Iarwain Ben-Adar; meaning "old, without father"
8. He did not disappear
9. Sing a rhyme that he taught them
10. Run naked on the grass

## QUIZ 63

1. Rúmil
2. *Feänor; Feänórian* tengwar
3. The horizontal groups of tengwar letters representing different modes of articulation
4. *Hwesta*
5. Right
6. Hobbit
7. Híni Ilúvataro
8. Remmirath
9. Apanónar; the "after-born"
10. Hrivë in Quenya and Rhîw in Sindarin

## QUIZ 64

1. Green-leaf
2. Thranduil; the king of the Wood-elves
3. The bow
4. Green and brown
5. That Gollum had escaped the Elves
6. "Deep they delved us, fair they wrought us, high they builded us; but they are gone"
7. "The Song of Nimrodel"
8. Arod
9. Sea gulls
10. Ithilien

## QUIZ 65

1. Lórien, the dwelling of Irmo and the place of repose of the Valar
2. By climbing a ladder
3. White
4. Celeborn's hair was silver; there was a "Tree of Silver" (also called Celeborn) in Tol Eressëa
5. Finarfin and Eärwen
6. Melian, the Maia
7. Celebrian; Elrond
8. Galadrim; "tree people"
9. Altariel
10. Egladil

## QUIZ 66

1. e
2. g
3. h
4. a
5. j
6. d
7. i
8. c
9. b
10. f

## QUIZ 67

1. h
2. f
3. e
4. b
5. i
6. d
7. a
8. j
9. g
10. c


## QUIZ 68

1. Because of the rumors of the evil Rider or Hunter started by Melkor
2. One, two, three
3. Saruman, the White; Gandalf, the Grey; and Radagast, the Brown
4. True
5. Some of Gandalf's fireworks for Bilbo's eleventy-first Birthday Party
6. Southlinch
7. Nobottle
8. False; copyright 1974 by Joy Hill
9. The purse belonging to William the troll and Gurthang, Túrin's sword
10. White and pale green

## QUIZ 69

1. He was a Maia of Aulë
2. Gorthaur
3. Angband
4. With a vision of his wife Eilinel
5. As a hostage of Ar-Pharazôn
6. Annatar, the Lord of Gifts
7. In Orodruin, the Mountain of Fire
8. At the fall of Númenor
9. In Dol Guldur
10. As a huge shadow shape that was blown away by a great wind

## QUIZ 70

1. Elwing, the wife of Eärendil
2. Malbeth, the seer
3. Ulmo
4. Treebeard (when he was sleeping)
5. Elrond and Círdan
6. Gilraen, Aragorn's mother
7. Gandalf, according to Gwaihir
8. Frodo, Sam, Merry, Pippin, Aragorn, Gandalf, Boromir, Gimli, and Legolas
9. The Istari
10. Aragorn

## QUIZ 71

1. An informal group of friends in Oxford made up of writers and scholars to which Tolkien belonged
2. On Tuesdays, they met in a pub called The Eagle and Child; on Thursdays, they met in the rooms of C. S. Lewis in Magdalen College
3. Manuscripts
4. Owen Barfield
5. C. S. Lewis's brother, Major Warren Lewis
6. *The Notion Club Papers*
7. Gervase Mathew
8. Mystical and supernatural "thrillers"
9. He did not care for them
10. Númenor, spelled "Numinor"


## QUIZ 72

1. The wilderness of Dungortheb
2. A Maia
3. Dancing
4. Tinúviel; "nightingale"
5. Celegorm and Curufin; Celeborn
6. Speak
7. They changed shape
8. One of the Silmarils in his iron crown
9. His hand containing the Silmaril was bitten off by the monster-wolf Carcharoth
10. The halls of Mandos

## QUIZ 73

1. Alf
2. The Twenty-four Feast
3. He swallowed it in a piece of the Great Cake
4. After it had fallen out of his mouth on to his hand, Smith clapped his hand to his forehead, without thinking
5. Eleven
6. Not one was the same as any other that grew on that tree
7. A Living Flower he had brought back from Faery
8. "The time has come. Let him choose"
9. He was Smith's maternal grandfather
10. That he was the King of Faery


## QUIZ 74

1. Wingfoot
2. On the hill of Cerin Amroth
3. Gollum
4. Strider
5. The daughter of Elrond and Celebrían
6. Estel; "hope"
7. An elf-stone (or *elessar* in Quenya)
8. Mid-years Day, 3019 TA
9. To decide the time of his death
10. The hill of Cerin Amroth

## QUIZ 75

1. English Language and Literature
2. Brithiach, Arossiach
3. Ægidius de Hammo (Farmer Giles of Ham)
4. Illuin
5. Clue finder, the web-cutter, the stinging fly; lucky number
6. My consent and cooperation
7. *Olvar*
8. *A Hobbit's Holiday*
9. Lightfoot's foal, swift Snowmane
10. Dorwinion


## QUIZ 76

1. a
2. b
3. d
4. j
5. i
6. h
7. c
8. f
9. g
10. e

## QUIZ 77

1. He tried to undo everything that they built
2. Utumno
3. Illuin and Ormal
4. Tulkas
5. For three ages
6. Ungoliant
7. Fëanor
8. He took them to Middle-earth and set them in his iron crown
9. As tall as a tower, clad in black armor with an iron crown and bearing a vast sable shield and Grond the Hammer of the Underworld
10. Húrin

## QUIZ 78

1. Golfimbul, who had his head knocked off with a club by Bullroarer Took, thus inventing the game of golf
2. A strain of orcs bred by Sauron in the Third Age. They made good soldiers because they were almost as tall as men, had strong legs, and did not weaken in sunlight
3. The Red Eye
4. "Slave," used as a term of derision for lesser Orcs
5. Treebeard
6. The Uruk-hai from Isengard who captured Merry and Pippin
7. *Glamhoth*
8. From captured Elves
9. Grishnákh
10. Frodo's coat of mithril-mail
11. Gundabad

## QUIZ 79

1. Curunír
2. White
3. The Dúnedain of Gondor
4. 2759 TA
5. A *palantír*
6. He hoped that if Sauron was not disturbed, the One Ring, which he coveted, would be revealed
7. They shimmered and changed colors when he moved
8. The Ents of Fangorn Forest
9. Sharkey
10. A gray mist, like a pale shrouded figure, rose from his body and was blown away by a wind from the West.


## QUIZ 80

1. Sauron
2. The tower of the city of Minas Tirith
3. *Barad*
4. Amon Súl and Annúminas
5. Narchost and Carchost
6. Belthil and Glingal
7. The Two Watchers
8. The men of Gondor; Minas Ithil
9. Unbreakable stone
10. The Tower of Avallónë on Eressëa which could be seen from Elostirion in the Tower Hills

## QUIZ 81

1. The giant in *Farmer Giles of Ham*
2. Radagast
3. Ar-Pharazôn
4. Thorin
5. Elrond
6. Elrond
7. Gimli
8. Sauron
9. Sam
10. Sam

## QUIZ 82

1. a
2. a
3. b
4. a
5. b
6. a
7. b
8. a
9. b
10. b

## QUIZ 83

1. Eöl
2. Ereinion; "scion of kings"
3. The Laiquendi, Elves who remained in Ossiriand after the death of Denethor; so-called because they wore green
4. A Nandorin Elf of Doriath, chief counsellor of Thingol
5. Eregion
6. Celebrimbor
7. *Telain*
8. Galadriel
9. Maglor
10. The Teleri

## QUIZ 84

1. 1937
2. The Revised Edition
3. 1960, 1965, 1969, and 1964, respectively
4. *The Oxford Magazine*; February 15, 1934
5. 1954, 1954, and 1955, respectively
6. Fourteen
7. 1968
8. *Redbook*
9. *The Dublin Review;* January, 1945
10. 1968 and 1967, respectively

## QUIZ 85

1. d
2. c
3. d
4. c
5. b
6. d
7. a
8. c
9. c
10. c

## QUIZ 86

1. One hundred and forty-four
2. At sunset
3. The six-day week called Enquië
4. *Coranar* (astronomical reference) and *loa* (seasonal reference)
5. The Reckoning of Rivendell
6. *Yestarë*
7. Six
8. Summer, fading, and stirring, respectively
9. *Quellë*
10. Three middle days not included in the seasons

1. A painting of a huge imaginary tree with branches and leaves in detail and glimpses of landscape beyond it
2. His lame neighbor, Mr. Parish
3. The Inspector of Houses and the Driver
4. Because he had no luggage
5. Two Voices, one severe and one more gentle, discussing his case
6. The words, "gentle treatment"
7. To a beautiful country spot, without a railway station, where his bicycle awaited him
8. The sight of his Tree, the one he had painted from imagination—now a real tree!
9. A corner of the canvas containing a beautiful Leaf by Niggle
10. Niggle's Parish

**QUIZ 88**

1. Tar-Ancalimë
2. Amandil, the father of Elendil
3. On the mountain of Meneltarma
4. Twenty-three
5. Because of their immortality
6. The King's Men and the Elendili, or Elf-friends
7. Adûnakhor
8. Míriel; Ar-Zimraphel
9. Nine
10. Isildur and Anárion

## QUIZ 89

1. The Mitheithel and the Bruinen
2. Amon Dîn, Eilenach, Nardol, Erelas, Min-Rimmon, Calenhad, and Halifirien
3. The Ringló was a tributary of the Morthond, in Lamedon, Gondor
4. Kheled-zâram
5. Ekkaia
6. Imloth Melui
7. The Lonely Isle
8. The three tall mountain peaks behind the Hornburg
9. An island in the lower part of the Withywindle
10. Greenwood the Great


## QUIZ 90

1. Randel Helms in his book *Tolkien's World*
2. *Good News From Tolkien's Middle Earth* by Gracia Fay Ellwood
3. "Beowulf: The Monsters and the Critics"
4. *A Tolkien Compass,* essays edited by Jared Lobdell
5. C. S. Kilby, author of *Tolkien and The Silmarillion*
6. Paul Kocher's book *Master of Middle-earth*
7. Robert Foster and J. E. A. Tyler, respectively
8. Marquette University
9. "Writers for the Seventies"
10. An honorary Doctorate of Letters

## QUIZ 91

1. Rayner Unwin, age ten, at the request of his father, publisher Stanley Unwin
2. C. S. Lewis
3. *Chicago Tribune* review of *The Two Towers*
4. "It is hard to believe that it will not eventually find a permanent place in Literature."
5. Peter S. Beagle
6. Richard Burton
7. *Catcher in the Rye* by J. D. Salinger, and *Lord of the Flies* by William Golding
8. Richard Adams
9. John Gardner
10. He had read the Tolkien biography by Humphrey Carpenter


## QUIZ 92

1. It was scribbled by Tolkien while he was correcting examinations
2. Replicas of Telperion and Laurelin made by Turgon in Goldolin
3. Udûn
4. That they had "clever brown fingers"
5. Tyrn Gorthad
6. Eärendil as a star
7. Mushrooms
8. The Misty Mountains
9. Baranor
10. The twelve-hour day of the Valar

## QUIZ 93

1. f
2. c
3. i
4. a
5. b
6. g
7. h
8. d
9. e

## QUIZ 94

1. Christmas 1920
2. "By gnome-carrier. Immediate haste!"
3. 1928
4. The North Polar Bear
5. The Red Elves
6. Ilbereth the Elf
7. It fell on the roof of Father Christmas's house when the North Polar Bear tried to climb it
8. Elvish letters
9. A Goblin alphabet
10. Christmas 1934

## QUIZ 95

1. "The Mewlips" and "Perry-the-Winkle"
2. William Elvin
3. Donald Swann; *At the Drop of a Hat*
4. George Sayer
5. *The Lord's Prayer* . . . in Gothic!
6. Band 3, side A, second album; band 15, side B, first album; band 7, side B, first album; and band 10, side A, second album, respectively
7. Band 6, side B
8. In 1952, two years before the publication of *The Lord of the Rings*
9. W. H. Auden
10. "Of Beren and Lúthien"

## QUIZ 96

1. Ghân-buri-Ghân, chief of the Woses
2. Gálmód
3. The second line
4. Gandalf
5. Éomer
6. The only child of King Théoden, killed in the First Battle of the Fords of Isen
7. She disguised herself as a man, calling herself Dernhelm
8. With *athelas*, the healing plant
9. He was crushed under his horse Snowmane
10. He followed Saruman and eventually came with him to the Shire

## QUIZ 97

1. Dick Plotz
2. Elvish graffiti in a New York City subway station
3. Many Tolkien fans came in contact and other Tolkien groups developed
4. "Frodo Lives!"; "Gandalf for President"; "Support Your Local Hobbit"; "Go, go, Gandalf!"; and "Come to Middle-earth"
5. The Fellowship of the Ring
6. The exchange of "mathoms"
7. The Mushroom Roll Race in which contestants push mushrooms with their noses to the finish line
8. *Orcrist* and *Mythlore*
9. In 1972, it was merged with the Mythopoeic Society
10. In 1968, by Vera Chapman

## QUIZ 98

1. h
2. f
3. c
4. d
5. b
6. j
7. i
8. g
9. e
10. a

## QUIZ 99

1. *Atendëa*; "double-middle"
2. By doubling the *loëndë*, the middle day of the year
3. The King's Reckoning
4. *Aldëa*
5. In mid-winter
6. *Nénimë*, the month of water; and *Súlimë*, the month of wind
7. *Yavannië*, named after Yavanna
8. *Asta*
9. *Lótessë* and *Ringarë*, respectively
10. *Yestarë*, *loëndë*, and *mettarë*


## QUIZ 100

1. Near the southern boundary of Mirkwood
2. *Galenas,* or *sweet galenas*
3. Ghân-buri-Ghân
4. Yellow
5. Máhanaxar
6. Haldir
7. *Translations from the Elvish*
8. Sigismond
9. The Nauglamír
10. Six
11. A Swan-ship